Tracker

Outcasts, Volume 3

Cyndi Friberg

Published by Anything-but-Ordinary Books, 2018.

This is a work of fiction. Similarities to real people, places, or events are entirely coincidental.

TRACKER

First edition. August 29, 2018.

Copyright © 2018 Cyndi Friberg.

Written by Cyndi Friberg.

Chapter One

Determined to remain calm despite the harrowing circumstances, Sara Sandoval took a deep breath and looked around. There were only two doors in this strange room, and she'd already tried both. One led to a lavish bedroom and the other was securely locked. There was no handle or triggering mechanism on the inside, no way to pry the door open. Shoving against the thing had gotten her nowhere. Sara's current captor might not be as overtly threatening as her predecessor, but clearly Sara was still a prisoner.

The walls, even the ceilings, were rough-hewn stone. Had this lair started out as a natural cave, or had the elves excavated the entire area?

Elves? Even in her head the word sounded ridiculous. Until a few hours ago, she'd thought elves were fictional characters in fantasy novels and movies, or plump little pointy-eared cartoons that sold fattening cookies on TV. Then her small group of friends had been attacked by the very beings who weren't supposed to exist. The attack had been so sudden and so strange that she was still struggling to believe it was real.

Maybe she shouldn't have been surprised. Life in general had stopped making sense about a year ago. After decades of secretly observing Earth, a group of aliens—yes, real live aliens—Rodytes they were called, casually revealed their massive spaceships and announced that they had an outpost inside the moon. Sara had always known the moon was hollow, so she felt vindicated by the sudden turn of events. She'd also been fascinated by how similar the aliens were to humans, and yet how different. Rodytes were larger than humans, their rugged features and muscular bodies immediately appealing. Yet they were aggressive, almost savage, despite their advanced technology. She'd never admit it, of course, but she found their alpha tendencies just as attractive as their handsome faces.

Sara had just about adjusted to the idea of interacting with peaceful aliens when a group of renegades called Outcasts rounded up and kidnapped several thousand human females. The Outcasts were burned-out mercenaries determined to establish a society of their own. They insisted their settlement would be free of prejudice and corruption, a place where everyone could thrive as long as they worked hard and obeyed the seven rules outlined in the Outcast Charter. Apparently, thou shalt not kidnap human females didn't make it onto that all-important list.

The Outcasts couldn't build this outlaw utopia without mates, and humans had the unwelcome privilege of being genetically compatible with all sorts of humanoid species. So that was how Sara and her friends ended up on this seemingly uninhabited planet. Only trouble was, the planet wasn't uninhabited at all. It belonged to a group of cave-dwelling elves. If that sequence of events wasn't enough to make someone doubt their sanity, Sara couldn't imagine one that would.

Shaking away the counterproductive thoughts, Sara continued her visual inspection. In contrast to the primitive setting, the furnishings were rich, even elegant, and there were overt indications of sophisticated technology everywhere. Their rescuer/captor, a female elf with long iridescent hair, had accessed this suite with a palm scanner, which triggered the motorized door. Lighting in the rooms, and in the corridors, was shaped like torches, however the flames weren't real, more like holograms. Sara had only seen a few rooms and several passageways, but she suspected there was much more to this underground labyrinth than anyone but the elves knew about.

Why would a technologically advanced society live in caves like animals? None of this made sense.

"If they're going to kill us, I wished they'd just do it," Heather muttered. "I'm so tired of being afraid."

"It could be worse. If we'd been kidnapped by ogres we'd be marinating right now. Or dwarfs. Aren't dwarfs the ones who—"

"Oh my God! How can you joke at a time like this?" Color came back into Heather's cheeks and spirit flashed in her blue eyes.

"Humor is my coping mechanism. If I don't laugh, I'll totally lose it. Would you rather watch me fall apart?" Heather had been assigned to Sara's cabin aboard the *Viper* a few days ago, so they didn't know each other as well as Sara's other two cabin mates. Lily and Thea had been together since leaving Earth, which had been five, maybe six weeks ago.

"I'd rather be back on Earth where my life wasn't threatened at every turn." She sounded almost petulant.

"No one is going to hurt us," Sara insisted. "The female elf won't let them."

"How will the female elf keep the males from hurting us if they come back with reinforcements? The guy with the greenish-blue hair looked really pissed. I doubt he'll let this go."

Sara sighed. Heather might be a perpetual pessimist, but there was truth in what she said. The teal-haired male elf had been leading the group who kidnapped them from the forest and he'd been furious when the female elf intervened. He was bigger and stronger than the female, so why had he allowed her to interfere? The female must be important, a leader of some sort.

After a short pause, Sara said, "I wonder if the female elf is the same one Arton has seen in his visions."

Disbelief scrunched up Heather's pretty face, then she shook her head. "You honestly think Lily's mate sees visions?"

A similar expression twisted Sara's face, but for an entirely different reason. "How can you still doubt it? Arton warned everyone about the elves days before anyone else saw them."

Heather shrugged. "I suppose."

Obviously, Heather was in denial, so Sara gave up on the conversation. There had to be some way out of here, or at least something they could use as weapons. A sofa and three contrasting chairs had been arranged in front of a rather ornate fireplace. The intricately sculpted hearth and mantelpiece looked out of place in this primitive room. A dining table and matching chairs were arranged against the far wall while a small desk and chair rested near the door leading to the bedroom. Everything was neat and orderly yet highly decorative as if the pieces had been brought here from some fabulous palace.

"Why do *you* think they took us?" A hint of challenge crept into Heather's tone and she pushed to her feet, though she stayed close to the corner. Having a stone wall at her back seemed to give her a sense of security.

"Haven't you heard? *Earth girls are easy.*"

Heather just rolled her eyes, so Sara answered the question honestly. "With the male, I think we were a power play. The elves want us off this planet, so they were going to threaten the Outcasts with our safety, even our lives."

"Oh my God," Heather cried. "You think they're going to kill us?" Her eyes widened and color drained from her face again. It must suck to have red hair and the paper-white skin that often went with it. Every emotion Heather felt was broadcasted by her complexion.

"I didn't say that." Heather was six years younger than Sara's twenty-eight years, but the difference had never seemed so glaring. Sure they were in danger, but hysterics never helped anyone.

"You said the female will keep us safe, but you're wrong." She shot past Sara, crossing the room in an agitated jog. "She insisted that she's our enemy! She looked at us like she wanted to strangle us both. That female is more dangerous than the male! And you..." Her hands folded into fists and she glared at Sara. "You don't know what you're talking about."

Heather's confusion was understandable, but why was she so angry? Worse, she seemed angry with Sara. "Do you blame me for this?"

"No," she snapped much too quickly. "Well..." Rather than completing the sentence, she averted her gaze.

What the hell? "How in God's name is this my fault?"

Without looking at her, Heather spoke in a low, shockingly hostile tone. "If you hadn't been determined to gawk at those shirtless Outcasts, we wouldn't have been in the forest today. I wanted to stay in the commons, safely inside the ship."

Sara just stared at the side of Heather's face, dumbfounded by the ridiculous conclusion. Sara had not been the only one enjoying the view. The Outcasts were building a barracks and the workers frequently stripped off their uniform tops when the heat became oppressive. She'd seen Heather's gaze focus on the construction site across the river more than once. Lily and Thea might be happily bonded, but Heather was still waiting for her potential mates to court her, and Sara was determined to reject all seventy-two of hers.

Guilt trickled through Sara's annoyance. She'd suggested the location and Heather indicated her uneasiness about leaving the ship. Several guards and a couple of humans had been attacked by huge, armored cats while hiking through the forest, so everyone had been cautioned to remain close to the Wheel. That was what the Outcasts called the structure they'd created by arranging twelve identical ships together like giant pieces of pie. Next they'd fitted each ship with enclosed walkways, allowing people to pass from one ship to the next without touching the ground. Though it looked rather odd, it worked quite well and made the ships—and more importantly the females—easier to protect.

Unless those females went into the woods so they could lust after shirtless males.

"I'm sorry," Sara said. "Obviously, I had no idea this would happen."

Heather sighed and finally looked at Sara. "I know you didn't, but that doesn't change the fact that—"

The main door slid open and they both swung toward the opening. Sara expected their captor, but a smaller, prettier female entered carrying a tray full of food. The sides of her pastel-blue hair had been pulled back and braided while the rest hung loose and silky to her waist. Like the other elves Sara had seen, this one had white skin and features so delicate they appeared almost doll-like.

She glanced at the humans, then crossed the room and set the tray on the dining table. Sara had just about dismissed her as a delivery person when the elf reached into the pocket of her dress and took out a small vial. Okay, what the hell was inside the vial? The elf unscrewed the tiny cap and picked up one of the glasses off the tray, then poured the contents of the vial into the glass.

Seriously? If she was going to drug them, she should have done it where her intended victims couldn't see what she was doing. Hadn't she ever seen a spy movie?

The blue-haired elf poured a small amount of pinkish liquid into the glass and swished it around, then crossed to where Heather stood and offered her the glass.

"I'm not an idiot," Heather sneered and turned around, presenting the elf with her back.

The elf said something, her tone pleading, but Heather was having none of it. Instead, she moved to the dining table and sat down.

Plainly frustrated by Heather's refusal, the elf crossed to Sara. "*Biren wanta.*" She lifted the glass toward her own mouth and motioned as if she would drink. "*Saun. Ro. Fee.*" She stressed each word or syllable as if speaking slowly would help Sara understand her language.

Each of the human females had been injected with a translator gizmo shortly after they were kidnapped. It allowed them to communicate in Rodyte, but other languages required additional uploads to the basic unit. It was doubtful elfin was even in their language database.

When Sara still didn't take the glass, the elf sighed heavily. "Not is bad."

Okay, that sounded almost like English. Was she trying to say the drug wouldn't harm her? "But what does it do? Make me sleepy?" She pressed her hands to her face and closed her eyes, making soft snoring noises. The elf laughed, so Sara opened her eyes. Just to make sure they were actually communicating. She pointed to herself and said, "Sara." Then pointed to the elf.

"Arrista," the elf provided.

The word was pretty enough to be a name, but how could she be sure? "English? Are you trying to speak English?"

"Yes." She nodded enthusiastically. "Bad but English."

Sara smiled, hoping to encourage her. "Your name is Arrista?"

"Yes, Arrista name mine."

Okay, that was definitely a reply. "What's in the glass?"

She seemed to think for a moment, likely searching for the correct English words. "Talk." She paused again, then said, "You talk Sarronti."

Sarronti was what Arton called the elves. Was she saying that drinking the liquid would allow her to speak their language? Was it a magic potion or some sort of technology? She'd seen scanners and holographic controls in the underground fortress, so chances seemed about fifty-fifty. "Are you sure it won't hurt me?"

"Yes, not hurt you."

"Don't do it," Heather insisted hurrying over to where they stood. "You have no idea what she put in that glass."

"If they wanted us dead, we'd be dead," Sara argued. "If she wanted to drug us, she wouldn't have done it right in front of us."

The elf watched them closely but said nothing.

"Make her drink some first," Heather suggested.

"Me talk Sarronti," Arrista replied, another clear indication that this was about communication not poisoning.

Nothing ventured, nothing gained? With a frustrated sigh, she made her decision. "All right, I'll do it." Sara held out her hand and Arrista gave her the glass. The liquid was cool and fruity, sweet but not cloying. Arrista motioned for her to finish it, so Sara drained the glass. Her pulse accelerated. Had her trust in Arrista been misplaced? A few minutes passed as the other two stared at her.

"Do you feel anything?" Heather asked, looking concerned rather than smug.

"No. Nothing."

They waited another minute or two and then Arrista said, "*Meltin tranfor tarke ia* moment more. Can you understand me now?"

"That's bizarre. I still hear your language, but I know what each word means." Sara shook her head, eyes wide and filled with wonder. "How is this possible?"

"Translation *lenitas*. I believe humans call them nanobots or nanites."

"How do you know that? Have you been to Earth? I understand that nanites are doing the actual translation, but someone had to teach your software English. When and why did your people interact with mine?"

Arrista glanced toward the doorway, her delicate features tense and unsure. Was she afraid someone would catch her talking with the prisoners? "The Sarronti have interacted with humans for hundreds of years. But humans fear what they don't understand and often become violent. So the Sarronti began to alter their appearance and blend into human societies. Many live there still."

"Do the Sarronti have spaceships or... How do you get back and forth from Earth?"

An enigmatic smile was Arrista's only response. Then she returned to the original topic. When and why had she learned about Earth? "Lady Isolaund's grandparents were a couple such as I described. They lived on Earth for many decades, changing their strategies as humans evolved. Lady Isolaund grew up on stories of their adventures, and dreamed of one day joining them on Earth."

"Lady Isolaund?" A shiver raced down Sara's spine as she thought of the female who had originally come to their rescue. "Is that the female who took us away from the teal-haired male?"

"Yes. She is very powerful and can be horribly cruel. Do *not* defy her."

Sara nodded, taking Arrista's warning to heart. Yet this glimpse into Isolaund's personality left Sara with a bunch of new questions. "So Lady Isolaund learned English so she could visit her grandparents. When was she last on Earth?"

"Her grandfather promised to send for her, to allow her to visit for an entire solar cycle once she was old enough to make the journey. That is when she learned your language, and also when I was given *lenitas*. Ladies of her designation do not travel without a companion. So we both studied human cultures and customs in preparation for our adventure on Earth."

If Isolaund was so fascinated by Earth, why was she so hostile? "Did you ever make the trip?"

Arrista lowered her gaze with a heavy sigh. "Her beloved grandparents were murdered by an inebriated woman who should not have been operating a vehicle. Isolaund's fascination with all things human turned instantly to bitter distain. It does not matter which emotion my lady feels, she feels them all intensely."

It wasn't fair to blame an entire race for the actions of one, but it was understandable. Many would have reacted the same way. "How long ago was the accident?"

"Thirteen solar cycles, or human years. My lady is very slow to forgive."

"That's tragic, and clearly your lady was devastated, but it doesn't excuse her attacks on my people. We had nothing to do with the incident."

Arrista's only response was a solemn nod.

They had drifted far off course, so Sara narrowed the focus of her mental ramblings. Start with communication. What were the *lenitas* capabilities? Would she be able to read as well as speak Sarronti? "Will other Sarrontians be able to understand me now?"

Arrista smiled patiently. "We are the Sarronti, not Sarrontians. And any Sarronti who has *lenitas* will be able to understand you, but only after their *lenitas* create a connection with yours. No one will command their *lenitas* to do this unless they know you have ingested them, so this can remain our secret."

That made sense, and there were obvious advantages to her captors not knowing she understood what they were saying. "Do the Sarronti interact with a lot of other species, or is it just humans?" That seemed rather arrogant, unless there was some sort of connection between the two worlds.

Arrista just motioned toward the table. "Your meal is getting cold."

Sara nodded and moved toward the table. She wasn't really hungry but it seemed rude to refuse.

As she passed Arrista, the elf caught her upper arm and Arrista's expression turned intensely serious. "You must tell no one what I have done. I would be severely punished if Lady Isolaund realizes you can understand us."

"I will say nothing. You have my word. But what does she want with us? Why did the male take us in the first place?"

Arrista shrugged, but secrets lurked within her crystal-blue eyes. "I know only what Lady Isolaund tells me, which isn't much anymore."

"But the male? Who is he?"

A violent shudder shook Arrista's narrow shoulders. "Lord Toxyn Jow. He is not nearly as important as he believes he is. The Guiding Council will not be pleased by his actions. They do not want war with your people."

Sara started to ask more questions, then changed her mind. Arrista had risked enough already just to give Sara this advantage. "Thank you."

She nodded once, then stressed again, "Don't let her know you can understand our language. I am the only one who could have made this so."

"I won't." Arrista started to leave, but Sara stopped her. "Why are you helping us?"

Looking back at her, Arrista's eyes filled with pain and something darker, maybe shame. "I know what it's like to be powerless. Those of my designation have no control over anything." She said nothing more as she hurried from the room.

"Wait! What about me?" Heather cried in a soft but urgent tone. "I want to be able to understand them too."

"You didn't want to communicate with her," Sara pointed out, and Heather went back to glaring.

"What did she tell you?" Heather asked as she wandered back toward the dining table and the food waiting there. "She jabbered away forever."

Sara's mind was still whirring with all the info Arrista had given her. "The female leader's name is Isolaund. The male who originally took us is Toxyn Jow. The female is every bit as powerful as she looks, but the male has an exaggerated concept of his true worth. However, Arrista called them lady and lord, so I think they both have some authority."

"Arrista? Is that the one who just left?" Heather returned to the seat she'd occupied briefly and slid the tray closer to her.

Sara nodded. She moved to the table as well, but rested her hands on top of one of the chairs rather than pulling it out. "Arrista didn't know why Toxyn took us, but he didn't have permission from their Guiding Council. He's probably in big trouble."

"Maybe they'll order Isolaund to free us once they find out we're here." Despite her apparent interest in the food, none of it had made it onto the plate she'd set in front of her.

"That would be nice." Sara didn't want to be pessimistic, but she thought their chances of being freed were pretty damn slim. "Oh, Arrista will get in horrible trouble if anyone realizes she gave me the translation nanites. You can't mention it, and I can't react to anything they say in Sarronti."

Before Heather could reply, a disruption erupted in the corridor. Deep voices shouted, though their words were too distorted for Sara to understand. Then she heard the distinct thuds and clatter of a violent altercation. Suddenly, the door slid open and a massive, armored Sarronti warrior stomped into the room. He was burly as well as tall, and his hair, which was dark gold like antique coins or heirloom jewelry, had been cut short, accenting his brutal features. Damn he looked mean. His amber gaze was sharp and assessing.

"Where is she?" he demanded in Sarronti.

Sara stared back at him as if she hadn't understood the question.

He stalked toward her and grabbed her arms, giving her a firm shake. "Where is Lady Isolaund?"

She quickly lowered her gaze and allowed her fear to show. "Please don't hurt me. I don't know what you're saying."

Just as abruptly as he'd grabbed her, he shoved her away. She rubbed her bruised arms, but silently thanked God that was all the enraged warrior had done.

The door slid open again and Isolaund stood framed in the opening. "How did you get in here?" Her tone snapped with resentment and anger as she glided into the room. "Where are the guards I stationed outside this door?" She motioned toward the door that had just slid closed behind her. "Explain this intrusion immediately."

The elves scowled at each other and spoke in their lilting, almost musical language. Thanks to Arrista, Sara understood every word.

The male elf turned on Isolaund with the same lethal calm he'd used on Sara. "I told you to stop going above or your curiosity would blow up in our faces."

His even tone and nearly expressionless features seemed to calm Isolaund. Her shoulders relaxed and she tossed back her hair. Iridescent color rippled through the knee-length strands. Sara had never seen anything so beautiful. Like Arrista's, Isolaund's features were sculpted and well proportioned, but there was a hardness to Isolaund's face that didn't exist in the younger elf. Arrista's eyes had been pale blue while Isolaund's were colorless. They shimmered like faceted crystal or priceless diamonds.

"My refusal to heed your warnings is what caused you to attack my guards and force your way into my private chambers?"

So the rooms belong to Isolaund. Sara had figured as much, but it was nice to know for sure.

"They have my son," the male sneered the admission between clenched teeth. "You sent your lackey above to snatch a couple of females and—"

"Toxyn acted alone," Isolaund snapped, soft pink staining her pale cheeks. "I had nothing to do with this. And last I checked, Toxyn was yours to command, *General* Alonov."

He moved so fast his image blurred and Sara gasped. Suddenly his fist was tangled in Isolaund's hair and her head was tilted way back. He towered over her, face a mask of rage and barely suppressed violence. "You might browbeat the council and terrorize everyone with your ridiculous cats, but it takes more than insolence to intimidate me. I went off to war with your father when you were still playing with dolls. Show some godsdamned respect!"

She stumbled back a step as he shoved her away, then her head snapped back to its haughty angle. Those diamond-bright eyes gleamed dangerously for just a moment before she gained control of her expression again. "I apologize for my disrespect, but what I said is true. Toxyn acted alone. I had nothing to do with his decision to take prisoners."

"Toxyn isn't smart enough to think this up on his own." The general dismissed the suggestion with an impatient wave of his hand. "What really happened up there? Did you send him on a recon mission and he decided he wanted to play with a couple of human females instead?"

She strolled across the room. Her movements seemed casual, but she put as much distance between herself and the volatile general as possible. "Why are you so certain I had anything to do with this?"

"Because Toxyn is a fool and we both know it. If he was aboveground causing trouble, he was doing so because you sent him. Now stop mincing words and tell me what happened."

She smoothed down the back of her hair, a hint of irritation showing in her tense expression. She stood in front of the fireplace now, shoulders squared, chin slightly raised. "He was supposed to burn down whatever that is they're building near the river."

Sara's eyes widened, so she quickly turned her head. They hadn't been Toxyn's target. As the general said, Toxyn had seen some helpless females and couldn't resist. What a bastard!

"The Outcasts captured Farlo during their interaction with Toxyn, so now they've got a problem with me." The general's voice became a menacing rumble.

"Farlo, your youngest? I didn't realize he was old enough to serve?" Isolaund's voice softened, so Sara looked at them again. The table was at her back, which meant Heather was as well, but the elves were far more interesting right now.

"He has only served for two moon cycles. I can't believe this is happening." Suddenly the fearsome general was gone and a worried father had taken his place. His broad shoulders sagged and the lines creasing his face seemed to deepen. "If they harm him in any way…"

"They won't," Isolaund insisted, but she kept the breadth of the room between her and the general. "He's a bargaining tool, nothing more. They want their females back, and they know the only way to make that happen is to offer an exchange."

"Or find one of the entrances to our world and start slaughtering everyone they encounter until they find their precious females." He shook his head, expression hardening again. "You're too young to remember the Roriton raids, but I'll never forget."

Sara shivered. No wonder these elves were leery of strangers.

"The Outcasts are not the Roritons," Isolaund said with sudden conviction. "They're surprisingly devoted to their females. They will agree to the exchange."

"Offer one, see how they react. I would like the opportunity to question the other before she's returned."

Isolaund didn't look happy about the suggestion. "I doubt they'll accept, but I'll make the offer."

The general's gaze swept over Heather, lust and cruelty smoldering in his amber gaze. "I want the red one, but I won't endanger my son to have her. Offer to trade for the dark one and make them believe it's the only offer they'll get."

"Of course." Isolaund was obviously trying to conceal her reaction, but a hint of resentment bled through. Maybe she had a soul after all.

"We'll speak again tomorrow." Without another word General Alonov left.

How were they triggering the door? There was no palm scanner and they hadn't used a voice command. Sara had tried everything!

"Who leads the Outcasts?" Isolaund asked in English as she moved slowly toward the table.

Sara paused to see if Heather would speak, but as usual she remained in silent-watcher mode.

"His name is Kage Razel," Sara told Isolaund. "The others call him Overlord."

"And the one with silver hair, what do the others call him?" She didn't halt her ambling progress until they stood toe to toe.

"Depends on the day." A hesitant smile bowed her lips, but Isolaund's expression didn't soften. Sara hesitated to reveal too much. Isolaund might have protected them from Toxyn, but she'd made it clear from the start that they were enemies. "He likes to be called Arton the Heretic, but the Rodytes also call him a harbinger."

"What are Rodytes?"

Maybe if she answered some of Isolaund's questions, the elf would return the favor. There was no harm in providing general information. Was there? "Rodytes are from a planet called Rodymia. Most of the Outcasts are hybrids, a mixture of Rodyte and other nearby races."

Isolaund's face revealed no reaction or emotion. All of these elves had incredible poker faces. "And harbinger? What is this?"

This information wasn't quite as general as the other, so Sara tried to downplay the importance. "They claim he can see the future." She waved dismissively. "I've never seen any evidence that he actually can. It's just a rumor." Except Arton had known about the elves long before anyone actually saw them. She also knew for a fact he was a strong telepath.

A strange little smile parted Isolaund's lips, then she motioned toward the table behind Sara. "Why are you not eating?"

Sara shrugged. "Don't have much of an appetite. Being kidnapped will do that to you."

Isolaund chuckled. "I'll make your stay as quick as possible. Have something to eat."

The door slid open and Arrista returned before Sara could repeat that she wasn't hungry. The younger elf moved immediately toward Isolaund. Thankfully, Isolaund moved toward Arrista too, which gave Sara a minute to catch her breath.

"They know about Weniffa, mistress." Unshed tears swam in Arrista's eyes and her panic seemed real. "They're going to kill her. We must do something quick!"

"Where is she?" Isolaund demanded sounding nearly as upset as Arrista.

Who was Weniffa? Did Isolaund have a daughter? If so, who was about to kill a helpless child? Sara took several deep breaths, forcing herself not to react to their obvious fear. *You can't understand them. You know nothing.*

"I moved her to my room, but that won't fool them for long. We must get her out of the Underground. The council is determined to teach you a lesson in the cruelest possible way."

Dear God. Did these elves really murder children to teach their parents a lesson? Her stomach cramped and her lips began to tremble. She pressed them together until they stopped.

Isolaund fisted her hands, and cried out in exasperation, "Even if I hide her above, she will not stay there. She knows the way back too well."

The child must be relatively old if Isolaund was considering hiding her aboveground by herself. It didn't matter! Even at twelve or thirteen, a child was helpless.

"Send one of them." Arrista motioned toward the two humans. "Tell them the cost of their freedom is to care for Weniffa. Tell them you will check on her wellbeing and if you ever find her abused or neglected, they will pay a horrible price."

Suddenly Sara detected cunning in Arrista's expression. What the hell was going on?

Isolaund was too upset to hear the hint of insincerity in her servant's voice. Was Arrista trying to help free one of them? Had she arranged this "crisis" for their benefit? Carefully keeping her expression bland, Sara remained silent and let the drama play out.

"Which should I send?" Isolaund gestured toward the table without taking her gaze off Arrista. "Did either attempt to communicate with you?"

"The dark one did. She is bolder than the red one, more compassionate too. I would send the dark one. She will be a much better protector."

But that left Heather alone down here, with general what-shisname panting after her.

"You." Isolaund motioned Sara over. "Arrista will take you to the surface, but it will cost you two things."

Sara swallowed hard, already hating herself for what she was about to do. "Please send Heather instead."

Isolaund narrowed her gaze, looking irritated and surprised. "You don't want to be free?"

"Of course I do, but I saw how that soldier looked at her. Heather needs to leave more than I do."

Isolaund scoffed and tossed back her hair. "General Alonov will happily shift his focus to you if your red friend is gone. He craves the novelty of bedding a human. Are you willing to take her place for that as well?"

Suddenly Heather was right beside Sara, squeezing her arm. "Please, Sara. I can't stay here. Let me go instead." Now Heather was on the verge of tears and Sara wanted to scream. Why did everything have to be so complicated?

"I did not make the offer to the red one," Isolaund snapped, tearing Heather's hand away from Sara's arm. "You will go and go now! Arrista will explain the conditions."

Shit. She looked at Heather's panicked face and felt tears sting her own eyes.

"Please," Heather sobbed. "Don't leave me down here alone. Don't—"

"I said go!" Isolaund shoved her toward the door.

Sara tried one last time. "But, Heather—"

"I will protect your red friend as I have protected you. Go!"

Arrista took Sara's arm and pulled her out the door.

"I can't just leave her here. If that bully wants Heather, Isolaund won't be able to stop him. Toxyn might back down, but Alonov is different. You know I'm right."

Arrista made a soft, scoffing sound that closely resembled her mistress's. "You don't know Lady Isolaund."

They rushed down one corridor and then another. Sara quickly lost track of which direction they turned and had no idea where they were going. As she'd thought, the tunnels went on forever and countless rooms were situated off short passageways that branched off from the one in which they ran. The elf stronghold was massive, and its primitive appearance was a disguise concealing the true level of their technology.

"Who is Weniffa?" Sara asked as Arrista's pace began to slow. "Is she really in danger?"

"Yes. One of my friends told me the council intends to kill little Wenny. I was on my way to warn Lady Isolaund when I realized we could help each other." She dragged Sara down one final corridor and paused before a nondescript door. "Do you like animals?"

Sara scrunched up her brows. What did that have to do with anything? "I'm a vet tech."

Arrista shook her head. "I do not know what that means."

"I work at a hospital for animals. Most days I like animals more than people."

"Good." With a hesitant smile, Arrista carefully opened the door, and hurried Sara inside.

The room was tiny, even smaller than Sara's apartment, which she frequently referred to as her closet. There was a chair, simple desk, and a bed, held off the ground by a functional wooden frame. As her eyes adjusted to the dimness, she noticed something curled up on the middle of the bed.

"This is Weniffa," Arrista explained as she crept toward the bed. "She's the sweetest karron you could ever—"

"Karron? Isn't that...Weniffa is a *battle cat*?" Holy shit! Isolaund wanted her to rescue one of her battle cats? Sara's system lit up with the strangest combination of fascination and fear. "Why is the council out to get, what did you call her, Wenny?"

"We cannot let them find her," she said firmly. "Let's get above, and then I'll explain everything."

Sara hadn't actually agreed to take the cat, but already her animal-lover instincts were kicking in. Who would kill a baby animal just to torture their caregiver? That was as reprehensible as killing a child, well, almost.

Arrista slipped her arms under the blanket on which Weniffa slept. "This has her mother's scent on it. It helps calm her when she grows anxious. Karrons are very perceptive. Wenny might not comprehend all the details, but she knows something is very wrong."

The cat was still relatively small. She looked like she weighed ten, maybe fifteen pounds. Once Arrista had the cat bundled up in its mother's blanket, she passed her to Sara. "She needs to start bonding with you."

The cat was heavier than she looked. More like twenty pounds. All Sara got was a glimpse of dark brown, almost black fur and tufted ears before Arrista urged her toward the door. Not willing to risk waking the cat, they hurried without running. Luckily most of the distance to the surface had been covered before they picked up Weniffa. Sara had done her best to memorize their path and catalogue everything she'd seen as they hurried past. Unfortunately, all the corridors looked the same, carved-out stone with sporadic wood and metal supports. They'd passed at least ten larger chambers, but Sara hadn't been able to see how large or determine what purpose they served.

Arrista opened an ancient-looking door and motioned Sara out into the shadowy forest. As the elf carefully closed the door, it seemed to disappear into the foliage. Were they using some sort of masking technology, or was it simply effective camouflage?

Arrista quickly led her away from the well-hidden entrance. There were no paths, no indication of which way they were headed, yet Arrista obviously knew her way around. "You heard everything they said. Do I need to explain what Lady Isoland wants from you?"

"No. She expects me to convince the overlord to trade General Alonov's son for Heather, and take care of Wenny until she's old enough to survive on her own."

"Exactly."

"Do all the battle cats belong to Lady Isolaund?" Sara asked when Arrista didn't say anything else.

"Karrons don't 'belong' to anyone. They choose to follow Lady Isolaund because she has earned their respect."

Like an alpha wolf or the strongest female in a lion pride. Sara understood the concept. She just wasn't sure how a human would prove their worth to a group of predatory felines. Instead of debating the issue, she focused on the practical details of caring for a karron cub. "How old is Wenny? Does she eat meat? I know a good amount about Earth's big cats, but I don't know how that equates to karrons."

"She's twelve weeks old, has been weened, and she's a carnivorous predator. What else do you need to know? Keep offering her raw meat until she stops eating. Wenny knows when she's full. She has just begun to hunt rodents and other field animals. Encourage this, but she is not yet skillful enough to live only off what she hunts. You will need to feed her for at least four more weeks."

Sara shifted the karron, supporting her weight higher against her chest. "She's manageable now, but how fast will she grow. I've only seen karrons from a distance, but I've heard they're huge."

Arrista sighed and stopped walking. "She will require your assistance for two maybe three moon cycles. After that, she should be strong enough, and skilled enough, to survive on her own."

"Moon cycles?"

"What you call months, though it takes our moons slightly longer to cycle."

So approximately ninety days. She was willing to do it, but how would the Outcasts react to having a baby battle cat aboard one of their ships? She wasn't sure this was her decision to make. But Heather's safety, perhaps her life, depended on Sara convincing the overlord to make the trade and allow the karron to be fostered. God, what a tangle. "Why does the council want Wenny dead?"

"They don't care about the cub. They want to prove their power over Isolaund. She has a tendency to stir up trouble and they're determined to put her in her place. The easiest and most effective way of hurting my mistress is to harm one of her cats. She is utterly devoted to her pride."

"But how will the council justify killing an innocent animal?"

"Wenny is sweet. She is loveable and utterly passive. These characteristics are not desirable in a battle cat. She failed her final exam, so Lady Isolaund was supposed to turn Wenny over to the labor pool."

"Labor pool? That sounds horrible."

"It is. Retired battle cats, or those not aggressive enough to be used in battle, are trained as beasts of burden. Karrons are very strong for their size, which makes them useful in certain areas of the Underground, mainly the mines and expansion projects. Lady Isolaund's predecessor simply 'disposed of' the battle cats once they'd outlived their usefulness. The council reluctantly approved this alternative, but I'm not sure it's any better."

"Do the Sarronti choose to live underground or is there... Why do you do it?"

With a heavy sigh, Arrista raised her face to the sky. Moonlight filtered through the tree branches, and stars were visible in several places above their heads. "We have no choice. We were overcome by an illness meant to wipe us out of existence. Most died, but those who didn't were irrevocably changed. Sunlight makes us sick. If we are exposed for long, we die. Like it or not, we are creatures of the night and must forever hide from the daylight."

"When did this happen? How long have you lived underground?"

Arrista hesitated. "It is hard to remember you are my enemy. Are all humans as likeable as you?"

Sara smiled, but she was also aware Arrista had avoided the question. "You just caught me on a good day."

"I need to return, and you must get Wenny inside the safety of your ship. Your freedom can be revoked like this—" she snapped her fingers "—if anything happens to the cub."

"I get it. I'll make damn sure she's safe and well cared for." She quickly licked her lips, struggling to believe she was actually free. "What about Heather? How do I contact you if I can get the overlord to agree to the exchange?"

"Have the silver-haired male contact Isolaund. And it better be *when*, not 'if', the overlord agrees. General Alonov is used to taking anything he wants and your friend has caught his attention."

"I don't know how much sway I have with the overlord, but I'll do everything I can." Arrista started to leave, so Sara stopped her. "One last question. Which way is the Outcast settlement?"

A patient smile parted Arrista's lips and pointed to a shimmer barely visible through the trees. "That is the river that runs beside your ships. Walk the same direction the river flows."

"Thank you, and tell Lady Isolaund not to worry. I'll treat Wenny as if she were my own."

Chapter Two

Unwilling to accept defeat, Xorran Entor poured energy into his psychic receptors and scanned the forest surrounding him. Each minute the kidnapped females were at the mercy of the elves increased the chances that they would be harmed or psychologically damaged by the ordeal. He could hear the warriors shifting restlessly, waiting for him to lock onto a signal, any signal. They were armed and ready to take back the females, but first Xorran had to find an entrance to the elves' stronghold.

Xorran was a tracker, a psychic hunter who could identify, and usually follow, energy echoes left behind by emotionally charged events. So why couldn't he follow elfin energy? Over and over, he'd locked onto a pattern only to have it stop abruptly for no apparent reason. Either the elves could teleport, or there was some element to this forest that Xorran didn't understand.

"We're wasting our time out here in the dark." Torak finally said what the body language of his team had been shouting for the past hour. "Let's get some sleep and start again at dawn."

Clenching his fists so he could maintain a calm expression, Xorran turned and faced the other male. Not only did Torak Payne command the best ship in the Outcast fleet, he had earned the title warlord by defeating his predecessor, and every male foolish enough to challenge him.

Xorran nodded once, acknowledging the warlord's decision. "I'm going to take one last try at it and then I'll head back."

"You stay, I stay," Torak insisted. "The overlord doesn't want anyone out here alone."

"There's a slim possibility that you and your team are distracting me." It was more like their frustration and impatience were preventing him from meditating deeply enough to accurately assess the signals he was receiving, but he wasn't going to explain all that to the frustrated warlord.

Torak dismissed his men with a curt telepathic command. The communication occurred via networked implants. Still, the signals were exchanged mind to mind, which qualified them as telepathy in Xorran's book.

"You're stuck with me," Torak said once his men and dispersed. "There's a very real possibility some of those pointy-eared bastards are still lurking in these trees."

Xorran sighed, but didn't argue. He no longer had the power of the Rodyte military to back him up, so he tended to avoid conflicts rather than race into them as he'd done for many years. "There's more to tracking than sniffing the ground. Give me some space and try not to make a sound."

"Understood," Torak muttered and faded into the shadows.

He was still there. Xorran could sense him, but Torak stood quietly, attempting to give Xorran what he needed. Knowing the compromise was as close to solitude as he was going to get, Xorran closed his eyes and opened his mind to the rhythms of the forest. The agitated scurry of frightened creatures faded and random odors swelled to the forefront of his consciousness. Dank dirt and sweet flowers combined with pungent dung and...water.

His awareness suddenly shifted, locking onto the river. He felt the current, heard the soft burble of the liquid tumbling over rocks. Damp grass crushed beneath running feet, and then a shocking spike of fear stabbed into his brain. He gasped. The emotions he absorbed were never this intense. Someone was terrified.

"This way," he urged in a harsh whisper.

He ran, agilely leaping over bushes and fallen trees in an effort to reach the river as fast as possible. Was he sensing one of the women? It had to be. Why would an elf be this afraid? He locked onto the signal, determined not to lose it as he'd lost so many in this strange forest.

Crashing through a tangled wall of underbrush, he emerged on a sloping riverbank as a small black animal dove into the water. An agitated human was right behind the animal and—much to Xorran's shock—she ran right in after the animal. She gasped, then cried out as the cold water saturated her uniform from mid-thigh down. Her uniform was identical to the one Xorran wore. This was one of *their* females.

Still not understanding why she was chasing the animal, he slid down the grassy bank and ran beside the rushing water, keeping pace with the panicked woman and the struggling animal.

"Catch her! We cannot lose that cat."

Cat? Was that thing a baby karron? Where had she gotten a cat? The creature was swimming for all it was worth, but the current was strong, sweeping it farther downstream with each passing second.

"Grab her!" the woman yelled. "Please!"

She seemed almost panicked now, so Xorran shook away his confusion and rushed into the water, grabbing the soggy animal by the scruff of the neck. It yowled pathetically and latched onto his chest and shoulder with sharp little claws. He ignored the pain and turned just in time to see the female lose her footing and plunge chest-deep into the sweeping water. She cried out, arms flailing as she fought to get her feet beneath her again. Holding tightly to the cat with one hand, he quickly caught the woman's upper arm and dragged her to her feet. She grabbed the back of his shirt, so he wrapped his arm around her shoulders, steadying her as they waded to the riverbank.

The cat pressed its face against his neck, its entire body trembling violently. Xorran covered its small body with both hands, trying to comfort the animal as well as minimize the pull of its claws. The woman stood beside him, hands braced on her knees as she struggled to catch her breath.

"Thank God," she said in between pants. "I thought I'd lost her for sure."

The cat let out another yowl and burrowed closer to his body, its face still pressed against his neck. "Are *you* all right?" he asked the female. The river had been surprisingly cold given the warm weather, and she was dripping wet from the shoulders down. He looked her over as well as the darkness allowed while also trying to calm the cat. Undoubtedly winded and upset, the woman didn't seem to be in physical pain.

"I'm fine." She tossed back her hair as she straightened, inadvertently drawing his attention to her clingy uniform. The moonlight shone from behind her, the resulting shadows blurring her features. The shape of her body, however, was outlined by the silvery light. She had high, full breasts and a trim waist, then her hips flared, creating a lovely hourglass shape.

Her aesthetics were pleasing, but they didn't explain the hunger creeping through not just his body but his soul. He felt restless and needy, anxious in a way he'd never experienced before. She moved closer and awareness pulsed through him. He could almost feel the cool night air wafting across her skin and tightening her nipples as her breathing accelerated. Her gaze widened and her lips parted, but he couldn't see her clearly enough to discern the emotions driving her reaction.

"She's shivering," the female said softly. "Could you please..." She made a vague gesture with her hand. "Is your shirt still dry?"

"It was until I picked up the cat."

"I had her wrapped in a blanket, but it's either lying on the other side of the river or it's downstream somewhere. Does your shirt open down the front? Can you tuck her in next to your skin?"

His uniform top opened in front, but it was too fitted for what she had in mind. Instead, he passed her the cat and quickly took off his shirt. Then using it like a blanket, he bundled up the cat and took the swaddled animal back from the female.

"I didn't expect you to go shirtless," she protested, yet her gaze lingered on his bare torso, making his skin tingle with anticipation. "On second thought," she whispered, "carry on."

Needing a distraction from his rapidly hardening cock, he asked, "Why'd she take off on you?"

She shrugged, then wrapped her arms around herself. Was she starting to feel the cold, or did his new state of dress make her uncomfortable?

"She woke up a few minutes ago and just freaked out." He found her reaction to him more interesting than the explanation. Was she feeling this electric attraction too? "She jumped out of my arms and was off like a shot before I could do anything about it."

Torak tromped down the bank, disrupting the tension as he slid to a stop slightly back from Xorran. "What is that thing?"

"Good question." Xorran looked at the female. Her features were still shadowed, but her squared shoulders and raised chin managed to convey defiance. "What sort of cat am I holding and where did—? Never mind. Other questions are more important. Are you one of the women kidnapped by the elves?"

"Yes."

She said nothing more, so Xorran asked, "Where is the other female and how did you get away from the elves?"

"The elves still have Heather and the rest is a long story, one the overlord needs to hear. Can we please get to the Wheel so I can change into something dry?"

Her teeth chattered and Xorran realized the cat wasn't the only one shivering. Would she accept it if he unwrapped the cat and gave his shirt to her?

As if hearing Xorran's quandary, Torak whipped off his shirt and draped it around the female's shoulders. Her eyes widened as she stared up at him. He appeared massive and likely threatening in the moonlight. "T-thank you."

Xorran tensed. Aggressive impulses surged in response to Torak's nearness to the female. How strange. Xorran didn't consider himself jealous, so why did he want to tear the warlord apart?

"You said the elves still have Heather. Then you're Sara?" There was a silky quality in Torak's voice that Xorran had never heard before. The warlord pulled her long dark hair out from under his shirt, obviously in no hurry to move away.

"Yes, I'm Sara." She nervously licked her lips as she took a step back.

Torak lowered his arms, but continued to study her.

"Let's go," Xorran advised, trying to ignore the irrational surges of jealousy pulsing through his system. Each of the captive females was genetically compatible with at least one of the Outcasts. Xorran had yet to learn who his match or matches were. Notifications went out on a regular basis, but he hadn't had an extra minute to clear his backed-up com-queue. Did compatibility explain why he had a nearly overwhelming need to shove Torak away from her and beat him senseless? Was this female a potential mate?

As if sensing his sudden tension, the cat shifted, digging its claws deeper into his chest. He stroked its back and whispered, "You're all right, little guy. You're safe now."

"*Her* name is Weniffa, but she seems to prefer Wenny," Sara told him, her gaze closely following every move he made. "She likes you."

He chuckled. "She likes me more than the river. That's not saying much."

The cat raised her head and shook off the water, big blue eyes gleaming in her dark, furry face. Her cry sounded less traumatized now, but her claws were still imbedded in his flesh.

"Have I lost my mind, or is that a tiny battle cat?" Torak asked, moving closer to Xorran.

The cat hissed, batted at him with extended claws, then pressed its face against Xorran's neck. "She doesn't like you, warlord." Xorran fought back a smile, thrilled with the cat's decision. Suddenly the claw marks were worth it.

Torak turned on Sara, all silkiness gone from his voice. "I don't think your story can wait. We're not taking a karron to the Wheel. Not even a tiny one."

"We have no choice." She planted her fists on her hips and stared up at him, apparently unafraid.

Xorran's chest warmed and his pulse accelerated. He had yet to see her in detail, but it didn't matter. He admired her spirit and courage. Many females would be clingy and tearful after being kidnapped. Instead, she stood toe to toe with the warlord, insisting he back down. One thing became crystal clear in that moment. Xorran wanted this female, wanted her badly.

"How did you escape the elves and why do you have the karron?" Torak persisted, his stern tone demanding answers.

Xorran would have tried a different approach, but Torak was right. They needed to understand what was happening before they took a battle cat anywhere near the settlement. The cub might be relatively harmless, but what happened if her mother took exception to being separated from her cub? They'd already lost two guards and suffered multiple injuries thanks to the battle cats.

The borrowed shirt started to slip, so she brought it back up to her shoulders and held the sides together in front. "Wenny is part of the deal. I have to keep her safe and taken care of or Isolaund will drag us both back to the Underground."

"Isolaund is the female elf Arton has seen in his visions?" Torak obviously knew more about the elves than Xorran did. Not surprising. Torak was part of the High Command, the overlord's advisory board.

"Yes." Sara shivered, clutching the shirt with both hands. "Isolaund trains the battle cats. They're like children to her."

"If Isolaund was willing to release you, why did she keep Heather?" Sara's teeth were chattering again, so Torak reluctantly started walking. "Explain," he prompted when she didn't answer his question.

"The boy you guys captured is the youngest son of an elf general. The general is furious and terrified for his son. Isolaund agreed to trade Heather for the boy."

"First of all, the captured elf is no boy. He is a well-trained soldier. He might be young, but I assure you he's deadly," Torak argued. "As for a prisoner exchange, that's up to the overlord."

They reached the building site, which meant the Wheel was just around the river bend. Xorran sighed, knowing he'd soon be free of Wenny's claws. But Torak stopped walking and pointed to the half-built barracks. "A row of rooms at the back are enclosed. We'll leave the karron there."

"Then I stay too," Sara insisted. "I promised Isolaund that Wenny would not leave my sight. I mean to honor that promise, at least until she has settled in to her new situation."

Torak crossed his arms over his chest. The warlord was not used to anyone arguing with him, much less a small human female. "You need to change out of those wet clothes, or you're going to…"

As he spoke, she turned around and kicked off her shoes, then took off her soggy pants. Careful to keep his shirt covering her, she removed her uniform top and shoved her arms into the sleeves of Torak's shirt. She fastened the front, then rolled up the sleeves as she turned back around. "I'm not leaving Wenny." Just to make sure he understood her position, she kicked the wet clothes onto his boots.

The warlord stared back at her in stunned silence. Then his gaze narrowed and he took a step toward her.

Wenny came alive with sudden speed, retracting her claws and lightly dropping to the ground. Xorran frantically tried to catch her, but the karron was too fast. She positioned herself in front of Sara and growled. White teeth gleamed in the moonlight and tufts of fur stood up along her shoulders and neck.

Xorran chuckled, unable to resist the irony. The fiercest warrior in a group of ruthless mercenaries was being confronted by two unarmed females.

Torak squared his shoulders and pointed at the cat. "This is the reason that creature is not welcome in the Wheel. Karrons are vicious animals, even the tiny ones."

"I'll guard them," Xorran volunteered.

"I still need to speak with the overlord," Sara reminded.

"We can com him from here," Xorran told her.

She shook her head, determination gleaming in her eyes. "This requires an old-fashion face to face. You won't believe everything I learned while I was with the elves."

"See if he'll agree to come here," Xorran suggested.

Torak acknowledged the idea with a terse nod and headed for the Wheel.

"We need dry clothes and clean blankets," Sara yelled at Torak's back. "Maybe something to eat!"

Torak didn't reply, but a break in his angry strides indicated he'd heard the directives.

There were fewer trees now, and Xorran could finally see her face. She had big, dark eyes and delicate features. Her face was too sophisticated for pretty, and striking fit her better than beautiful. Torak's shirt engulfed her body from neck to knees, but he could still remember her curvy shape outlined in the moonlight. He desperately wanted to see it again, without the distraction of her uniform this time.

"Are you always this feisty?" Xorran asked with a lazy smile.

"Just when people piss me off." She tossed her head and bent down and scooped up Wenny. "Damn it, you're still wet."

Xorran handed her his shirt, which was also damp. She turned the damp side out, then wrapped it around the cat. "She's likely warmer than you are," he pointed out. "I understand why you did this, but you are in danger of catching cold out here."

"So are you." She motioned toward his pants with her chin, unable to use a more conventional gesture with her arms full of squirming karron. "You should take off your pants too. I assure you, I've seen a naked man before."

Her casual suggestion took his semi-erect cock to full attention so fast he had to stifle a groan. Was she serious?

When he just stared at her in stunned silence, she laughed, the sound wonderfully light and musical. "I'm kidding. All you guys take yourselves way too seriously. You can even have your shirt back if you want it. If we get out of the wind, Wenny will be fine without it."

"I'm used to the cold." It wasn't a lie. Rodyte soldiers were trained to endure all sorts of hardships. Inclement weather was an annoyance, nothing more.

"Is Rodymia colder than Earth?" She walked into the barracks, looking around curiously at the skeleton-like structure. The karron had calmed somewhat. It seemed less squirmy.

"Rodyte soldiers are desensitized. It prepares us for all sorts of extremes."

She flashed a playful smile. "Then you are Rodyte. I can't see you that well, so I wasn't sure."

He tensed. "I am half Rodyte, and half Bilarrian."

"Ah," she muttered. "Battle born?"

"Does it matter?" he snapped. "Would you feel more comfortable if my mother were from Mejikon rather than Bilarri?"

She seemed to shrink right before his eyes. Her shoulders sagged and she lowered her gaze. "I obviously struck a nerve. Forget I brought it up. Your past is none of my business."

Xorran sighed. He was being a jerk and he wasn't sure why. She'd been friendly, almost flirtatious and he bit her head off. He lightly touched her arm, drawing her to a stop. "I'm sorry. This night has been extremely frustrating. I didn't mean to take it out on you."

Her smile returned, though it wasn't quite as enthusiastic. "You called him warlord, so I presume that was Torak Payne. But I don't know your name."

Thinking back, Xorran realized neither Torak nor he had introduced themselves, even after they asked her name.

"Damn," he muttered. "We were both being rude. I'm Xorran Entor. Please call me Xorran."

"You're the tracker," she mused. "Is that why the night was frustrating, because you couldn't locate the elves?" Not waiting for his answer, she started walking again.

Everyone seemed to know about his abilities now and it felt very strange. He'd spent half his life trying to hide the fact that he had access to his magic. "I'd latch onto a signal, and then it would just stop, ending for no apparent reason. How did you get to their stronghold? You said something about the Underground."

"The entire stronghold is underground. According to Arrista, they can no longer tolerate the daylight. It's literally toxic to them."

He nodded. Ever since Arton introduced the idea of other inhabitants on the planet, everyone had been speculating on how they stayed hidden and why they would hide. Xorran had been a fan of the underground city concept. It simply made the most sense, as did an extreme intolerance to ultraviolet light. "Can they teleport? Is that how they took you underground?"

She shook her head. "We climbed down a ladder on the way in and the floor just angled up on the way out."

Then why in all of hells' torments couldn't he find even one of their entrances? They must be using some sort of illusion or holographic camouflage, or if the legends about elves were based on fact, some sort of magic shield.

They reached the back of the barracks and Xorran opened the door to one of the enclosures. And that was all it was, four walls, a wooden floor and half-finished ceiling. As much as

Wenny liked water, things could get interesting if it started to rain.

"Be it ever so humble," Sara muttered under her breath. "I hope Torak took me seriously. Staying here will be pretty miserable without some basic supplies."

"If he doesn't return in a few minutes, I'll wake one of my friends and have them bring supplies out to us."

"Sounds like a plan." Cradling the cat with one arm and keeping the oversized shirt under her with the other, she carefully sat down. Then she stretched her long legs out in front of her and rested back against the wall. "I guess if the overlord doesn't drop by tonight, I can make an appointment with him tomorrow. But I really don't want to leave Wenny alone." She hesitated for a second before asking, "Will you stay with her?"

"Of course I will, but the overlord will probably come. You have firsthand information about our enemy."

She acknowledged his statement with a nod, then asked, "Can you swing the door shut? I'd like to let her go."

"Of course."

He closed the door and tried not to stare at her, but he couldn't drag his gaze away. She sat in a pool of moonlight streaming in through one of the open sections in the roof. Her long dark hair was tousled and fatigue shadowed her eyes, and still he found her beautiful. This had to be the pull. He'd heard about the urgent need that engaged whenever a Rodyte male encountered a compatible female. But he hadn't understood how different it felt from ordinary lust. He didn't just want to share pleasure with her—though that was definitely a big part of what he was feeling. He wanted to protect her and provide for her, ensure she lacked for nothing as long as she lived. He wanted to *mate* with her.

Sara carefully opened Xorran's shirt and freed Wenny. The karron cub shook her entire body, fluffing out her dark fur. Even in the dim light her eyes appeared blue as she looked around the unfamiliar room. Then she crept around, sniffing everything, including Xorran. He reached down and scratched behind her ears and Wenny rubbed against his calves. The tracker had made a friend, and it fascinated Sara to see so large a male being so gentle.

"Do they grow armor, or is it implanted once they're fully grown?" Xorran asked.

"I don't know. They didn't tell me much about karrons, not nearly as much as I'd like to know if I'm going to be her new caregiver."

He looked at her, dark gaze gleaming in the moonlight. "If the cats are so important to Isolaund, why would she give one to the enemy?"

At first glance, she'd thought the warlord was better looking, but Torak's personality soon changed her mind. The warlord was autocratic and inflexible, basically a militant jerk. Xorran, on the other hand, was watchful, still assertive, yet willing to compromise. And Wenny liked him. Often animals were better judges of character than people. Lord knows Sara had gotten it seriously wrong a couple of times.

"If a karron isn't aggressive enough to be a battle cat, he or she becomes part of the labor pool," she explained. "Arrista said they're trained to be beasts of burden. Isolaund didn't want that sort of life for one of her babies, so she offered my freedom in exchange for rescuing Wenny. I'm also supposed to convince the overlord to exchange the captured elf for Heather. That should be everyone's top priority. I'm not sure Isolaund can keep her safe."

Xorran nodded, his expression thoughtful as he walked around the enclosure. His arms swung loosely at his sides and moonlight played across the curves and ridges of his muscular physique. It wasn't hard to imagine what it would feel like to run her hands over those same bumps and hallows, to press against him and arch up into him. God above, the man was a walking, talking fantasy.

He seemed even more restless in the confined space than Wenny. Like most Rodyte hybrids, his hair was dark. The sides and back were short, but there was just enough length on top to reveal its tendency to curl. His features were bold, overtly masculine, without being brutish. His eyes were dark, but the color of his phitons was lost in the shadows. Phitons were the strange luminescent rings that separated a Rodyte's irises from their pupils. The irises were almost always dark, but the phitons came in all sorts of colors, red, blue, purple, green, even silver and gold.

Xorran stared past her for a moment, then announced, "The overlord is on his way, and he doesn't sound pleased with this development."

"He's not pleased that I'm free and unharmed. Wow, that's awesome."

"Sara, for the most part, Kage Razel is reasonable and will listen to all the information before making a decision. But you need to dial back the defensiveness, or all you're going to accomplish is making him angry."

She sighed, knowing he was right. But pressure was closing in on her from every side. The overlord would doubtlessly want to know everything she'd learned about the Sarronti, while the Sarronti wanted her to campaign for the release of the general's son. Isolaund expected her to care for Wenny, but the Outcasts didn't want a karron anywhere near the settlement. And lastly, Heather stood on the sidelines, ringing her hands, terrified that the elf general would rape her. They all had legitimate needs, and they were all looking to Sara to fulfill them.

What else was new? Her parents ran a group home for abused and neglected children, and she was their eldest biological child. People had been looking to her for solutions her entire life.

The overlord arrived a short time later, carrying a compact solar lantern. With his strange, asymmetrical hairstyle and penetrating eyes, he looked even meaner than Torak. Sara scrambled to her feet, feeling vulnerable on the floor. Wenny scampered toward her and growled softly at the overlord. She wasn't as insistent as she'd been with Torak, but the overlord's dark gaze immediately shifted to the cat.

"So you're what all this fuss is about?" He bent to one knee and held out his hand, palm down. Wenny cautiously sniffed his fingers, looked at him, then gave his knuckles a gentle lick. "That's right, girl. I'm no threat to you." He pushed back to his feet, towering over Sara.

She looked at Xorran, not even sure what she expected from him. His phitons were purple. The light from the overlord's lantern finally revealed their color. He didn't say anything, but he offered an encouraging smile.

The overlord glanced at Xorran, then chuckled as his gaze returned to her. "Do I need to take off my shirt in your presence? That seems to be the practice of my men."

"I'll make an exception for you." She felt her cheeks heat and instinctively averted her gaze. Authority emanated off the overlord as if he'd been born to power. Maybe he had. No one seemed to know very much about him.

"Torak told me you weren't harmed." He waited until she looked at him to ask, "Is this true? Are you okay? Not all wounds are physical."

Pleased that he cared enough to make his own determination, she nodded. "I'm fine, but Heather is still in mortal danger. We cannot leave her in the Underground."

"Rather than me asking a million questions, why don't you start at the beginning and tell me what happened tonight?" The overlord set the lantern on the floor, then surprised her again as he sat against the opposite wall and crossed his long legs at the ankle.

Had he realized she felt uncomfortable with him staring down at her? Kage Razel wasn't at all what she'd expected. Trying to match his nonchalance, she resumed her earlier pose, carefully covering her thighs with the oversized top. Wenny crawled onto her lap, kneaded her thighs for a moment, then lay down. The karron's claws barely penetrated the sturdy material covering Sara's legs, but she was glad when Wenny stopped and curled back into a furry ball.

Taking his cue from the other two, Xorran sat as well. He chose the wall directly across from the door. Had he just chosen a position that allowed him to see her and the overlord, or was Xorran demonstrating his neutrality?

"You and your cabin mates gathered by the river to catch up after Lily's absence," the overlord prompted. His tone was light, conversational, but his gaze remained sharp and assessing.

She quickly organized her thoughts, deciding which details to explain and which didn't really matter. "The attack came out of nowhere. I was being dragged through the forest before I even had time to scream." The overlord silently waited for more information, so she continued, "They took us down a ladder and into their underground fortress. I saw miles of passageways and many large rooms. The place is massive."

"How many elves did you see?"

"Twenty or thirty, but I have no doubt there are many more."

He nodded. Tension lifted his shoulders and thinned his lips. "I know you made a deal with Isolaund. How did that come about?"

A firm knock on the door postponed Sara's response. Wenny raised her head and looked around. Xorran rose and opened the door, admitting two Outcasts, each laden with supplies. The karron cub didn't seem to feel threatened by the intruders. She watched them silently from the security of Sara's lap, then closed her eyes and tucked her head under her paws.

"Did they get everything, her royal highness demanded?" the overlord asked with a lazy half-smile.

Sara felt a tiny pang of guilt about her attitude, but Torak had been a total jerk at the time.

Xorran sorted through the supplies, then nodded. "Our demanding princess will be pleased."

The overlord nodded to the newcomers. "Thank you, gentlemen."

They returned his nod, then gazed at Sara as they ambled toward the door.

Xorran watched the others, and his gaze narrowed, gleaming dangerously. If Sara didn't know better, she'd worry that he was going to fly across the room and pummel the other two. But why would he react that way? Xorran barely knew her.

"Back to your story," Kage prompted.

Shaking away the distracting interruption, she told him everything that had happened. She kept the information concise and factual. Both males listened intently and only interrupted when something she said didn't make sense to them.

"So Arrista turned me loose and your men brought me here," Sara concluded.

"Damn. You're one hell of a spy, even if you weren't trying to be." The overlord stood and rolled his shoulders. "This is more intel on the elves than we've managed to collect since we've been here."

She smiled, embarrassed by the praise. "They're very different than I expected. From what little I'd heard, I pictured Legolas running through the forest with his bow and arrow. The physical similarities are striking, but these are sophisticated beings with technology equal to, maybe even superior to, yours."

The overlord nodded thoughtfully, then asked, "Would you be willing to give us a sample of your blood?"

She tensed, unnerved by the odd request. "Depends why you want it."

"It's a shot in the dark, but it would be extremely beneficial if we could study one of the nanites you ingested."

Her eyes widened as trepidation renewed her chills. "Do you think they're harmful?"

"I don't think Arrista would have given you something harmful. The Sarronti have interacted with humans before, so she would know if their tech was incompatible with your physiology. Much can be learned by studying a culture's technology."

That all made sense, so Sara nodded. "You can have the sample."

"Good. Now I'm not opposed to trading Alonov's son for Heather, but there are a couple of complications."

"Other than Alonov having the hots for Heather?" Her voice thinned, revealing her agitation. Nothing was more important than Heather's safety. Complications be damned.

He glanced at Xorran, likely asking him something via the internal comlink all the Outcasts shared. The overlord didn't react outwardly to whatever they said and his intense gaze soon returned to Sara. "If we agree to the exchange, do you still have to foster the karron?"

Sara stroked the sleeping cub's back, feeling insanely protective. It was no longer an obligation. She wanted to take care of Wenny. "She isn't safe in the Underground. If Arrista hadn't been warned what the council was planning, Wenny would be dead already."

"Who suggested the barter, Arrista or Isolaund?" the overlord wanted to know.

"Arrista made the suggestion, but Isolaund immediately agreed. They both care deeply for the cats."

The overlord stroked his stubbly chin, expression thoughtful. "Arrista enabled you to understand their language and suggested a way for you to be freed?" He shifted his gaze back to Xorran. "Sounds like a potential ally to me." When Xorran only nodded, the overlord asked Sara, "Do you have a way to contact Arrista?"

She shook her head, belatedly realizing how helpful that would have been. "Arton is supposed to tell Isolaund what you decide, and the sooner the better."

The overlord nodded, seeming to mull over everything he'd learned. He took a couple of steps toward the door, then turned around and came back to where he'd started. "If Arrista is involved in the prisoner swap, it might be our only opportunity to recruit her."

Again he was focusing on all the wrong things. Rescuing Heather should be their only priority. "I think that's going to require a longer conversation than we'd be allowed at a 'prisoner swap.'"

Her pessimism had no effect on the overlord. "I was thinking more along the lines of passing her a note that said, meet me tomorrow at midnight."

Sara just nodded. Having a contact in the enemy camp would be smart and strategic. She just wasn't sure Arrista would become that contact. Despite her willingness to help Sara, Arrista seemed loyal to Isolaund. Rather than prolong the debate, she kept her opinions to herself.

"My primary hesitation is the general's son. We're not having much luck interrogating him." A hint of humor eased the tension from around his mouth. "It's hard to question someone when you don't understand a word he says. Would you be willing to work with one of our interrogators?"

"How long will that take? I can't stress it enough, Heather is in real danger." Whatever information they could glean from Alonov's son wasn't worth what Heather would suffer if the general got his hands on her.

"Four hours," the overlord proposed. "If we haven't gotten anything out of him in four hours, Arton will contact Isolaund."

"Two," Sara countered stubbornly. If she didn't champion Heather, it was obvious no one else would.

The overlord looked at Xorran and shook his head. "You're going to have your hands full with this one, tracker. The sooner you claim her, the better."

Sara gasped and snapped her gaze around to Xorran. "You're on my list of matches?" There were seventy-two names on her list and most of them had meant nothing to her. She tried to avoid interaction with the males. "Why didn't you tell me?"

"This is the first I've heard about it," Xorran objected.

Then why didn't he seem surprised?

"He's right," the overlord told her. "Torak said you were 'irrationally stubborn'. So I pulled you up in the matching database, thought one of your potential mates might help me negotiate. Come to find out, you've been with one all along."

"That's not too surprising," she muttered. "I've got seventy-two matches. But I was told all the males were notified."

Xorran didn't seem pleased by this fact. He stared at her silently, emotion gleaming in his purple-ringed eyes.

"Notifications were sent," the overlord told her. "That doesn't ensure that they're opened."

The last thing she needed was an aggressive male trying to seduce her and her own hormones sabotaging her at every turn. "This is all beside the point," Sara insisted. She carefully lifted the cub off her lap and placed her on Xorran's uniform top. The cat stirred for a moment, then went back to sleep with a groan. Fighting to keep her lower body covered, she maneuvered her legs under her then stood. "We have to rescue Heather. I'll help the interrogator for two hours, no longer."

Much to her surprise, the overlord agreed. "That should be enough time to know whether or not we're going to get anything out of him. Especially if your mate scans the elf while he's questioned."

Xorran stood as well, his features tense with displeasure. "I'm not technically empathic. My abilities—"

"Are close enough." Kage asserted. "If Arton digs around inside a mind, it always results in damage. Give us your best shot. That's all I ever ask."

Xorran's expression remained tight, but he didn't object. "She needs to change clothes and relax for a while before she's put in any more danger."

"I'm fine." Sara touched his arm and looked up into his purple-ringed gaze. "Yes, I need a new uniform, but I won't be able to relax until I know Heather is safe."

After a tense pause, the overlord nodded. "Put yourself back together and I'll meet you and Xorran on the detention level of the *Viper*."

"What about Wenny?" Sara lifted her chin, warning him that she wouldn't allow the cub to be neglected.

He chuckled and shook his head. "And I thought Thea was the troublemaker in your cabin." He stretched out his back and acquiesced with a chuckle. "I'm ready for a break. Xorran can escort you to the *Viper* and back. I'll hang out with Wenny." One of his dark brows arched in challenge as he added. "Will that suffice, your royal highness?"

With an unapologetic smile, she dipped into a curtsy. "Thank you, kind sir."

Chapter Three

A tentative tapping drew Isolaund's gaze toward the door separating her bedroom from the rest of her quarters. She had just retired for the night and sat on the foot of the bed, brushing out her long sliver hair. Only Arrista would dare to interrupt, so Isolaund called, "Make it quick. I'm not in the mood for drama."

The door eased open and Arrista peeked inside, her expression tense and filled with dread. "I'm so sorry, mistress, but General Alonov is here again, demanding to see you."

"By all that's blessed, is Alonov daft? There is nothing he can say that can't wait until—"

Arrista was shoved out of the way and Alonov burst into the bedroom. "I beg to differ! Are the reports true? Did you release one of the human captives tonight?"

Isolaund squared her shoulders and clenched her jaw. The man was a mannerless bully. "Get. Out." She didn't raise her voice. Instead, she infused each syllable with indignation.

He stomped toward her.

In an instant, Certice stood between them, teeth bared, snarling out an unmistakable warning.

He glared at the battle cat, then turned his hostile gaze back on Isolaund. "My spies just told me one of the humans was tromping around in the forest. Is it true? Did you release the dark one?"

"I told you I would negotiate the exchange. That's what I'm doing. We can discuss the details in the morning or—"

"I thought Toxyn was the fool, but his actions make more sense than yours!" He motioned toward her with such aggression that the karron snapped her jaws and growled even louder. He ignored the close call and focused on the female. "We had the upper hand. Why in all the gods' names would you give that up?"

"I did no such thing," she insisted, crossing her arms over her chest. "I sent a messenger, nothing more."

"That's nonsense and we both know it." Alonov's tone was calm, but cold. "I want the red one *now*. I'll see to the negotiations myself. You're dismissed."

Her chin shot up, but part of her wanted to laugh. "Sorry, General. I don't answer to you."

His fists balled at his sides and his nostrils flared. He glared at Certice, then sneered, "You love to forget the fact, but this little hobby of yours is a military project. With the snap of my fingers, I can reallocate your entire budget." Without another word, he stormed from the room.

Isolaund glared at the door through which he'd stormed. The bastard was right. When push came to shove, she worked for him. But everyone answered to the Guiding Council. And she had a closer connection to that *august body* than Alonov could ever claim. But would her brother help her? She sneered again. The only thing more frustrating than Alonov was those useless bureaucrats! And Indrex could be the worst of all.

Arrista appeared in the doorway a moment later, looking flushed and rattled. "Will he return?"

"Doubtful." Isolaund considered the question more carefully, but still came to the same conclusion. "He was just blowing off steam."

"Did you hear that they arrested Toxyn?"

Isolaund arched her brows at the news. "I hadn't heard, but I'm not surprised. Toxyn's misbehavior resulted in the capture of an Alonov. No one endangers a member of the Ayrontu without risking harsh punishment. Which is as it should be." Toxyn was Ayrontu also, but his family was not nearly as revered as the Alonovs. If someone with a lower designation had committed the crime, they would have been executed on the spot. The Guiding Council might want to blur the lines between designations, but centuries of tradition didn't change overnight.

"Of course, Mistress." There was a strange brittleness in Arrista's tone that Isolaund had never heard before. Arrista had been particularly moody ever since she spent the night with Toxyn. Did the girl regret her decision to offer her body to Toxyn? Yes, Isolaund had offered Arrista as a sexual surrogate when Toxyn pressured Isolaund for sex, but she'd made sure Arrista was willing before she left them alone. She searched the girl's tense features, then dismissed her concern. It must be something else.

Arrista started to leave, but Isolaund stopped her. "We need to move the red-haired human. Alonov will come for her tonight and I don't want him to find her."

"Of course, Mistress. Where shall I take her?"

Isolaund thought for a moment. Alonov's spies were everywhere, and he knew the forbidden passages even better than she did. There was only one place she knew of that would be safe from the general. "Can you find the grotto by yourself? You've been there several times with me." The grotto had once been a place of worship and sacrifice to sorcerers like her mother. Many believed powerful spirits still lingered there, so most avoided the secluded chamber.

"I believe so, mistress."

"Stash the human there, and I'll work with my brother to resolve this as quickly as possible." She hated to admit that she needed Indrex's assistance, but there was no avoiding it now. Indrex was her only weapon against Alonov. "Make damn sure the human is securely restrained. The grotto is far too close to the surface for my liking."

《 》

"THEY RELEASED MY LIST of matches almost a week ago," Sara said, her voice soft, almost sad. "Several of my suitors came forward right away. They seemed pleased and excited by the possibility of courting me."

Xorran tensed. If she was trying to make him jealous, she'd succeeded. "And how did you react? I was under the impression you wanted to resist us at all costs."

She shrugged. "I talked to the polite ones, explained my hesitation without being a jerk."

"Were some less than polite?" His hands clenched into fists. If anyone insulted or frightened her, he would make them regret their rudeness.

A mischievous smile tugged at the corners of her mouth. "I found creative ways to discourage the ones that wouldn't listen. I've always found it easier to laugh than get angry."

He looked at her, eyes narrowed. "Are you the one who dared Heftar to eat a *lonfan* pepper?"

Another shrug lifted her shoulders. "He was downright obnoxious. I refuse to regret how I handled that situation."

Hearing about Heftar's humiliation had made Xorran laugh, so he couldn't really chastise her. Heftar was known to be overly aggressive, even a bully. Doubtlessly he had earned the discomfort her prank had caused him. Xorran was pleased to know his potential mate had creative ways of dealing with such males.

"Why didn't you open your message?"

Her tone was tinged with disappointment, so Xorran looked at her. He'd hoped to read her expression, but her face was averted. "I've been extremely busy. Now that everyone knows I'm a tracker, requests for my time are endless."

"Then how did you know we were compatible?"

Following her example, he kept his gaze fixed on the wide riverbank as they walked along in the moonlight. "I sensed your fear more clearly than I've ever felt anything in my life." Her emotions hadn't reached him since. Still, he wasn't sure if she was really as calm as she seemed. He refused to invade her mind to satisfy his curiosity. "Once I was near you, it didn't take long to figure out why your emotions found me so easily."

She finally looked at him, big dark eyes luminous in the dimness. "But we aren't bonded. I thought the mind link is what allows couples to exchange thoughts and emotions."

For so long he'd been endangered by his abilities. It still felt strange to discuss them openly. "I'm mildly empathic. Tracking, in the Bilarrian sense of the word, is a specialized form of empathy. And empathy is always most effective with blood relatives and mates, or potential mates."

"I see," she whispered and averted her gaze again.

"Why does that make you uncomfortable?" He didn't smell arousal on her yet, though her natural scent was sure as hells affecting him. She wasn't oblivious to him either. He'd caught her gaze moving over his bare torso more than once. Still, the pull didn't usually engage for the female until the couple kissed. And gods how he wanted to kiss her, to bury both hands in her hair and slowly taste her sweet mouth.

"You already have access to your magic," she pointed out. "Why saddle yourself with a mate for the rest of your life?"

Stunned by her casual words, he stopped walking and faced her. Gaining access to their magic was an important factor in why battle born males wanted to bond with human females. Like most of the Outcasts, Xorran's mother had been a war bride, the Bilarrian captive of his Rodyte father. For several generations war brides had been forced to bear the children of their Rodyte captors in the hopes that the child, or children, would inherit their mother's magic. Daughters often manifested faded echoes of their mother's power, while sons were usually born latent. The practice of taking war brides had been outlawed, but that didn't keep the battle born males from searching for ways to access their full potential.

After many years of failure, a group of ambitious geneticists found a way to trigger the needed changes. By using the natural metamorphosis that occurred during mating as a delivery mechanism, the hybrid genome was much more likely to accept the necessary recoding. The final ingredient in the complex recipe was human females. Humans were resilient and tolerated genetic resequencing better than most species, so the scientists focused on tailoring the transformation program for a Rodyte hybrid male and human female.

Still, accessing their magic was one motivation among many. Outcasts, and their battle born comrades, longed for the stability and comfort of a soul bond. They wanted a loving female beside them as they built a future free of prejudice and violence. They wanted someone to love and protect, to share every new experience. Did none of that appeal to her? At some point in the not too distant past she must have been attracted to the concept. Why else would she have volunteered to bond with a battle born rebel?

"Is that how you see soul bonding? A 'saddle'? Something unwanted and cumbersome?"

"I don't know." She glanced into his eyes then quickly away. "The closest thing to soul bonding on Earth is marriage and I've never known anyone who could make that work. My parents hung on for thirty-one years and then had one of the nastiest divorces I've ever witnessed. It was ridiculous how horribly they turned on each other." Her voice softened, became wistful as she added, "It was also really sad."

Unable to fight his need to touch her, he covered her shoulders with his hands and moved closer. "Soul bonding is very different than any human relationship. Humans can lie and deceive, harbor resentments and plaster on fake smiles. Soul-bonded couples share everything, thoughts, emotions, aspirations and fears. There is no hiding, no falseness once the link is formed. It's honest, visceral, and real."

She twisted away from him and started walking again. "I don't think I want anyone to know me that well."

He tensed, easily keeping pace with her agitated steps. She'd volunteered for the transformation program back on Earth. That was how Arton and his team of hunters had known who to kidnap. Each female they'd taken—with a couple of exceptions—had already been tested and approved as a genetically compatible mate. How was this any different? "Did you volunteer for the transformation program?" Wanting an honest answer, he fought to keep the challenge out of his tone.

"Yes, but..." She sighed, still avoiding his gaze. "Everything that's happened since we left Earth has made me reevaluate my decision. Lily and Thea are *so* different now. It's hard to believe they're the same women I met six weeks ago. Thea's the one who convinced me that the only rational response to being kidnapped was to resist you guys at every turn. Now she's bonded to Rex and seems genuinely happy. I never thought I'd use that adjective to describe Thea Cline."

Confusion drew his brows together. "You don't want your friends to be happy?"

She shot him an impatient look. "Of course I do. But her transformation has been so sudden and so complete that it doesn't seem natural." She sighed and added, "It seems coerced, almost drug induced."

The Wheel came into view, so Xorran slowed his pace, not yet ready for the conversation to end. "How do humans behave when they've first located a potential partner? Are they not emotional and overly affectionate?"

"Yes, but not to the extent I've witnessed in Lily and Thea. They're like...Stepford wives."

"I don't understand the reference."

"It means spirited females who were secretly replaced by lifelike robots that behave exactly the way their husbands wanted their wives to behave. It comes from a classic sci-fi book and movie." Her steps paused and she finally met his gaze again. "I've seen humans that were head-over-heels in love. They can't keep their hands off each other and they're convinced they'll be together until their dying day. Then the newness wears off and time changes their bodies. Pretty soon they're bored and restless, and one or the other cheats. Or worse, money pressures and life just wears them down until there's simply nothing left. Whatever the cause, it never lasts. That's what scares me about Thea and Lily. A soul bond is permanent. What happens when the pull wears off and they realize there is no escaping what they've done?"

"Lily and Thea are not married to their males. They are soul bonded." He shook his head, frustrated by her vehemence. "You would have to experience the difference to understand."

She laughed and shook her head. "And experiencing 'the difference' requires a permanent commitment. Sorry, Xorran, think I'll pass."

There were ways for her to preview what it was like to be soul bonded, but he didn't argue. She was in no state of mind for romance. One of her friends was still in danger and they were about to face one of the beings who had terrorized her. Xorran's eyes narrowed. Was that why she was so defensive? Was she still afraid? It was so damn tempting to scan her mind and find out exactly what she was feeling. He shook away the temptation. One of the first lessons his mentor taught him was that power came hand in hand with responsibility. Xorran's abilities were meant to be passive. If he forced his power to penetrate another's mind, it corrupted his energy. Not to mention that it violated the other person's trust.

They reached the Wheel and walked up the ramp leading to the common area on the lowest deck of the *Viper*. With multiple seating arrangements and nutria-gen kiosks, the area was part lounge, part cafeteria, and a favorite gathering place for the human females. After passing through security scanners that detected various forms of weapons as well as identifying authorized passengers, they were met by one of the guards who handed Xorran a clean uniform top. The guard smirked, but departed without comment.

"Main medical is on deck three, aft, so let's go there first," Xorran suggested. "That way we won't forget later."

She looked confused for a moment, then understanding sharpened her gaze. "The blood sample. I'd almost forgotten."

"It will just take a moment," he assured as he quickly pulled on the shirt.

She watched him silently, dark gaze warm and filled with mischief. "What a shame," she whispered with a wicked smile. "I can finally see you clearly and they make you cover up."

Her playfulness sent a fresh rush of desire curling through his body. "We can stop by my cabin on the way back and I'll give you a private viewing."

She laughed, her cheeks turning pink. "I'll keep that in mind."

Main medical was bustling, as usual. Xorran found Doctor Foran and told him that the overlord wanted Sara's blood screened for nanites and any abnormality that might have resulted from their use. Foran agreed to do the tests, but directed one of his technicians to collect the sample. As Xorran predicted, the detour only took a matter of minutes.

The detention level was all the way in the forward section of deck two, and they'd entered through aft, so they still had a bit of a walk ahead of them.

Rodyte ships were built for functionality, not comfort. The mottled-gray corridors were long and unadorned, the decks textured, providing traction. They'd tried to make changes since arriving on the planet, hoping to provide their females with a more hospitable environment. The "commons" on deck one were the best example. The leisure area had once been a series of cargo holds.

"You don't have to question the elf directly," he said, hoping to lighten her mood. "You can simply translate for the interrogator."

"I'm not afraid of the elf," she insisted, tossing back her long dark hair. Her face had been scrubbed clean and color returned to her cheeks. She'd put on a clean uniform and combed out her hair before they left the barracks. He'd thought she was attractive before. Now he couldn't keep his eyes off her.

"I didn't think you were," he told her firmly. "But it might be easier to analyze the elf's reactions if you're not in the same room with him."

She shook her head and squared her shoulders. "I need to look him in the eye and show him that we won't be victims to their cowardly tactics. The Sarronti can't live above ground anymore, so there is no reason we can't share this planet."

"That's a valid point, but your ability to speak Sarronti is only an advantage as long as the Sarronti are unaware of it. If you confront this elf directly, you reveal your ability."

Pausing as if to absorb the implications, she slowly nodded. "And he'll tell the others as soon as he's released."

"Undoubtedly," Xorran agreed.

"I hadn't thought about that." A frustrated frown crept across her delicate features.

They lapsed into contemplative silence as they reached the detention area. As with most Rodyte ships, the area was one open space that could be divided into smaller spaces depending on how many people needed to be secured or interrogated. Opaque energy fields surrounded each enclosure, preventing any sort of communication with the outside world, and limiting interaction between the detainees. At present there were three prisoners, two from the *Viper*'s crew, and the elf.

"How will the elf understand the questions?" She paused and looked at him, a hint of challenge sharpening her expression. "I don't actually speak Sarronti. I can't tell the interpreter which words to use."

"How did you communicate with Arrista?"

"Her translator nanites linked with mine, but the nanites did the actual translation. I still spoke English and she spoke Sarronti. The technology just allowed us to know what the other was saying."

"So without this link, we're out of luck." He sighed. He'd hoped to spare her the stress of facing one of her attackers, but she honestly seemed to welcome the opportunity. "Do you know how to form the link?"

She shook her head, looking a little less enthusiastic. "I'll have to find a way to let the elf know I can understand him. Hopefully, he'll do the rest." Suddenly dread widened her eyes and drained the color from her face. "What about Arrista? If I reveal that I can communicate, Isolaund will know what Arrista did."

"Damn it." Xorran scrambled for a way to question the elf without endangering a potential ally, but nothing came to him. They couldn't communicate with the elf unless he linked with Sara, and finding out that Sara had Sarronti translator nanites implicated Arrista. It was all a giant circle of useless frustration.

"Give me a minute to update Kage. I'll see if he has any suggestions."

She nodded, looking as frustrated as Xorran felt.

He turned his head, unable to think of anything other than Sara while he looked at her. He quickly told the overlord what they'd realized and Kage suggested involving Torrin Havier.

"What did he say?" Sara asked as Xorran faced her again.

"Torrin Havier is on his way. I'm not sure why the overlord thinks an assassin can help with this situation, but he was adamant."

"An assassin?" She sounded uncertain and glanced down the corridor.

"Torrin is well known as a contract killer. He's wanted in more places than the overlord." Distracted by the possibilities, Xorran casually revealed the information.

"You don't sound like you know him very well. Can we trust him?"

Quickly marshaling his expression, Xorran chose his words with more care. He didn't want his confusion to make her even more uncomfortable. "I've met him, but I don't know any of the Outcasts well. I haven't been with them that long. The overlord wouldn't have suggested we network with Torrin if he wasn't trustworthy. The overlord knows how important this is."

She nodded, but pressed back against the wall and crossed her arms over her chest.

It felt awkward to loiter here in the hallway, but once they entered the detention area the elf would be able to see them. Xorran didn't want to appear as if they didn't know what they were doing, which at the moment was more or less true.

Torrin strode down the corridor a few minutes later. Even dressed in the khaki uniform worn by all the Outcasts, the assassin looked deadly. He'd combed his dark hair back from his face and bound it at the nape of his neck. The severe style accented his angular features and unusual gray/green eyes. His penetrating stare quickly swept over Xorran, then switched to Sara and lingered, though his expression—or utter lack thereof—didn't change.

"What's up?" Torrin's casual tone contradicted his lethal first impression.

"How much did the overlord explain?" Xorran asked.

The assassin shrugged. "Not much. We need to know whatever the elf is willing to tell us, but no one can communicate with him."

"Sara was given translation nanites while she was their captive. She can speak their language, but doing so openly endangers the elf who helped her escape." Xorran struggled to understand the overlord's strategy. What did he think Torrin was going to be able to do? They needed an interpreter, not an assassin. "I'm not sure why the overlord thought you could help us."

A sly smile bowed his lips as he ambled closer. "If you'll allow me to touch your female, I'll see if there is anything I can do."

Xorran tensed, instinctively moving in front of Sara. "Why do you need to touch her?" And how the hells had Torrin realized Sara was a genetic match with Xorran? He hadn't even kissed her yet. If her scent had changed, he would have noticed.

"*Where* do you need to touch me?" Sara moved to his side, her expression nearly as suspicious as his.

"Any skin-to-skin contact should allow me to scan for the nanites. I'll attempt to link with them, which may or may not allow me to access their translation programming."

The explanation did little to soothe Xorran's suspicions. "Are you battle born? I've never heard of this ability."

Torrin scoffed. "Says the Bilarrian tracker. Are *you* battle born?"

It was a valid point. Xorran's skills were just as atypical of battle born soldiers as the one Torrin described. Apparently they both had unusual backgrounds. "You can touch her hand or her arm. Nothing above the elbow."

"Seriously." Sara glanced at him impatiently. "If he touches me inappropriately, I'll slap him. You don't need to treat him like a criminal."

"I am a criminal," Torrin said without shame. "We all are."

Sara tensed at Torrin's casual statement. He hadn't sounded proud about it. He was just stating facts. Even if the Outcasts hadn't committed crimes before coming to Earth, each had been party to a mass kidnapping. She would be wise not to trust any of them. But why draw her attention to the fact?

"Is it your intention to harm me?" She countered his directness with the same, yet his reminder still left her feeling uncomfortable, vulnerable.

"Of course not. We want the same thing." He held out his hands, palms up. "If I can help you, I will. I simply won't know if I have anything to offer until I touch you."

She glanced at Xorran, but his hostile gaze was fixed on the other male. Typical. Rodytes were ridiculously territorial. "Is this where you two scratch the ground and bash your heads together?" Torrin smiled and the tension banding her chest released.

He lowered his arms and the smile faded. "I'm no competition to your tracker. Unfortunately, I'm not compatible with any of the human females."

Compassion smoothed Xorran's expression, but his gaze remained wary. "Did they tell you that before or after you agreed to join the Outcasts?"

"After, but I don't blame Kage. The overlord was more surprised than I was. Compatibility has been an issue my entire life. My physiology is unusual." There was a wealth of information in the statement, though Sara didn't understand the specifics. Pain shadowed Torrin's eyes until he blinked away the past and held out his hands again. "Ready?"

She took a step toward him and placed her hands on his. He slid his hands up and closed his fingers around her wrists. His grip was firm without being hurtful and a strange radiance appeared deep in his eyes. Trepidation spread through her and she tried to pull away. He held her securely as his being gradually sank into her mind. She struggled against the tingling rush at first, afraid of the strange sensations. But the initial uncertainty gradually gave way to fascination.

He moved agilely through her mind, searching, analyzing. She could sense the skill and intensity with which he worked. As he focused on one area, the tingling intensified. She gasped and instinctively tried to pull away again.

"Steady," he whispered and something swirled through his gaze like smoke. Distracted by the odd motion in his eyes, she stopped resisting long enough for him to locate the cluster of nanites. "There they are," he muttered. "Almost done."

The rings in his eyes blurred, stretching and swirling as the entire mass began to rotate. Shocked and afraid, she tugged against his hold on her wrists. "What are you? Rodytes don't... Where are you really from?"

"He's Ontarian, or least part Ontarian," Xorran explained. "Why pretend to be battle born?"

Torrin shook his head and released her arms as he came out of the trance. "My mother was a prisoner of war, just like yours. She just happened to be a hybrid. My maternal grandfather was Ontarian. Does that make my abilities any less advantageous?"

"I apologize," Xorran said. "Your background is none of our business."

"I'm not ashamed of it. It's just complicated enough to take over conversations, so I tend to avoid it."

Sara hesitantly touched his upper arm, drawing his attention. "Were you able to determine if you can help us or not?"

"I believe so. What do you think?" He spoke in slightly accented Sarronti.

"Wonderful." She smiled with relief. "Now you don't need me."

"Sorry, I'm not sure my range will hold if you leave the area." He sounded genuinely apologetic. "I'm accessing your nanites to perform this little parlor trick. If I lose the link, the ability will disappear."

"But I can't speak Sarronti," she pointed out.

A knowing smile curved Torrin's lips. "Actually, you could with a little practice. It's just a matter of channeling your thoughts back through the translator to retrieve the appropriate words. I can teach you how once your friend is rescued."

Sara nodded. Being able to speak Sarronti would enable her to communicate with the elves without allowing them into her mind. She glanced at the assassin, unsure if he was a safer alternative. "Do I need to be in the room with you? If the elf sees me, it defeats the purpose for involving you."

Torrin shook his head. "The link should hold if you watch from the control room. It shouldn't take long to find out what our reluctant guest knows."

Xorran led her to a small adjoining room from which the entire detention area could be viewed. The front wall of the room was one massive display that had been segmented into smaller images. Xorran greeted the two guards by name, but neither did more than glance at her. Did everyone presume she belonged to Xorran simply because they arrived together? The conclusion probably worked to her advantage, even if it was slightly annoying.

One of the guards pushed his hands into a holographic grid, known as a control matrix. With a few fluid movements, he filled the left half of the display with images of the elf from multiple angles.

"He's been sullen, almost pouty, since he got here," the same guard explained. "It's hard to know for sure, but I don't think he's very old."

"Has he spoken, attempted to communicate in any way?" Xorran asked.

The guard shook his head. "Just sits there with his hands fisted, staring straight ahead."

Now that she was safe and well-protected, Sara looked at the elf more closely. Sleek honey-gold hair angled across his forehead and framed his narrow face. The pointed tips of his elongated ears peeked out of the gleaming strands. Like his father, the elf had amber eyes and thick dark lashes. His body was long and lean, not yet filled out by maturity, and years of strenuous exercise.

An opening appeared in the opaque energy field surrounding the elf and Torrin stepped into the cell. The area seemed to shrink as his tall, muscular form filled in the empty space. His bearing was aggressive, gaze slightly narrowed.

"Are you in contact with your people?" he asked in Sarronti.

The elf's head snapped to the side and he shot to his feet. "You speak our language. How is this possible?"

Xorran touched her arm and asked, "What are they saying?"

She quickly told him.

"I'm asking the questions," Torrin said, his tone cold yet calm. "Answer honestly and you won't be harmed. What is your name?"

The elf's chin angled up and defiance burned in his amber eyes. "My father is General Cagor Alonov. If you know our language, you should know what that means."

"I didn't ask your father's name. I asked yours."

The elf licked his lips, his gaze nervously darting about. "Farlo. Farlo Alonov. I am Ayrontu, so I expect to be treated with the civility that requires."

Torrin glanced toward the camera providing the security feed. *Ayrontu? Do you know what that means?*

The word hadn't translated for Sara either, so she thought, *No clue. See if Farlo will explain.*

With a subtle nod, Torrin turned back to the elf. "Ayrontu has no English translation. What does it mean?"

One of the elf's brows arched dramatically. "You speak our language, yet know nothing about our designations?" He sniffed, then averted his face. "I will tell you nothing."

"Fine. A few days without food or water should change your mind." He took a step toward the door.

"Wait! Send word to my father and I'll tell you anything you want to know."

That was easy, maybe too easy. The elf wanted Torrin to think he was terrified, but sharp, cool cunning kept flashing in his amber eyes.

"Tell me something interesting and I'll send word to your father," Torrin countered.

"It is common knowledge, so I see no harm in telling you. We have six designations. Each is determined by a family's standing in the community. Ayrontu is the top designation. We are leaders, the families with wealth and power."

"What are some of the other designations?" Torrin wanted to know.

"Layot designates artisans and teachers, merchants and farmers. Their designation is the largest, most inclusive. Manual laborers belong to Witernel."

"What is the lowest designation?" Though his face revealed nothing, a hint of anger crept into Torrin's tone.

"Niffal."

"And who belongs to Niffal?" His anger was obvious now.

Farlo looked confused by Torrin's hostility. "Slaves and bondservants, though there are currently very few slaves. Does your society not have designations? You seem angered by the structure."

"The levels might not be quiet so defined, but I think most cultures have such designations." With his hands clasped behind his back, Torrin slowly approached. "Did your father order the taking of female prisoners?"

"No!" he all but shouted the word. "That was all Toxyn. We were supposed to cause trouble, start a fire or two. No one said anything about taking prisoners."

"Which one was Toxyn and why did you follow his lead?"

"He's designated leader of my team. I had no choice." His expression smoothed, though he still sounded defensive.

Torrin nodded. "And which one was he?"

"Toxyn has greenish-blue hair and is unusually tall for a Sarronti."

Sara translated the conversation for Xorran, feeling almost sorry for the elf. He was little more than a child, and Torrin was seriously intimidating.

"Will Toxyn harm the females?"

"No." Yet the elf's hesitation spoke louder than his denial.

Sara shifted her weight from one foot to the other as anxiety bubbled up inside her. Heather might be safe from Toxyn, but the general was another matter.

"What was Toxyn trying to accomplish by stealing two of our females?"

"He's a fool," the elf snarled. "He's so determined to make a name for himself that he doesn't care who he hurts in the process."

Challenge arched Torrin's brows. "And yet you said he won't harm our females."

"He won't be allowed to harm them. Once my father learns of my imprisonment, he'll take control of the situation. I guarantee you'll be dealing with him, not that idiot Toxyn."

"How many fighters does your father command?"

"Thousands." He glared and then amended, "Hundreds of thousands."

One corner of Torrin's mouth twitched, the reaction so subtle it was doubtful the elf noticed. An initial response was more accurate, and obviously Torrin knew. "Do you live below ground by choice or necessity?"

"We go where we will and live as we please." With each exchange, the elf's arrogance grew and his believability diminished. "You should pack up and leave this place before my father destroys you utterly."

Torrin indulged in a lazy smile, clearly amused by the elf's vehemence. "I thought Toxyn was the only Sarronti who makes war on women."

The elf just glared.

The smile gradually faded and Torrin's expression hardened. "We have a room onboard this ship equipped with ultraviolet light. It allows us to grow food while in space. How long will you survive if I lock you in the room?"

"You wouldn't dare."

"I promised not to harm you if you answered my questions honestly. I suspect you just lied to me. Care to change your answer, or shall I find out for myself?"

"Sunlight is harmful to us," the elf admitted after a tense pause.

"How harmful," Torrin persisted. "How long will it take you to die? A few days or a few hours?"

"My tolerance is stronger than most. I'd last a week or more."

Torrin accepted the information with a nod. "One of your females speaks English. How did she learn our language?"

For the next two hours Torrin questioned the elf. What little he revealed, Sara already knew, but it was nice to hear Arrista's information confirmed by a second source. Finally, Torrin left the detention area and joined them in the control booth.

"He's not going to say any more," Torrin concluded. "He might be young, but he's stubborn and prideful. He'll die rather than endanger his people."

Xorran nodded, his expression tight and thoughtful. "I know the overlord won't be thrilled with the outcome, but thanks for your assistance."

"Anytime." Without another word the assassin-turned-interrogator left.

"So what's our next move?" Sara asked.

Xorran shrugged, but his expression was anything but indifferent. A muscle twitched above his jaw and complex intensity smoldered in his dark eyes. "I guess Arton will contact Isolaund and propose the prisoner exchange."

"And in the meantime Heather remains at the mercy of General Alonov." Sara shook her head, frustration cutting through her helplessness. "We have to do more. There has to be a way to rescue her tonight."

Xorran moved closer and lowered his voice, though the effort was likely wasted in such a small room. "We searched every inch of that forest. The entrance or entrances are there. We just can't detect them."

Reluctantly, she agreed. "I couldn't see the exit we used seconds after we emerged from the Underground. They're using some sort of shielding technology, or they can literally cast spells."

"They will make the trade," Xorran stressed. "Heather will be back with us very soon."

Sara wanted to believe it. She just prayed "very soon" would be enough for Heather.

When they returned to the barracks, they found the overlord sitting against the wall, the karron cub curled up on his lap. The sight was so inconsistent with his ferocious reputation that Sara couldn't help but smile.

"Any luck?" he asked, absently petting Weniffa's soft fur.

Xorran responded before Sara could order her thoughts. "He confirmed a lot of what Arrista told Sara, but offered nothing new."

The overlord nodded and carefully eased the cub off his lap. "I'll let Arton know." He stood and paused to stretch out his back. "You two need to figure out how to control the cub in the morning. This place will turn back into a construction zone, so leaving her here isn't an option."

"Understood," Xorran replied.

"In fact, if returning her to Isolaund isn't an option, you need to come up with long-term strategies for her too. She'll need fresh meat and water, exercise and stimulation that doesn't include mauling any of us."

"Understood," she echoed Xorran's word, but didn't manage to replicate his calm tone. The thought of waiting around for Arton to contact Isolaund was giving Sara an ulcer. She could still hear Heather's terrified pleas as Arrista hurried Sara out the door. "Please let Arton know that time is of the essence. See if Isolaund will guarantee Heather's safety. I'm really worried about her."

"You focus on the karron. We'll take care of Heather. You have my word that she is my top priority."

His sincerity was small comfort in the face of all she knew. Still, she nodded and said, "Thank you."

The overlord left a few minutes later, leaving Sara alone with Xorran. She sat near the karron cub, positioning herself much as the overlord had sat.

Xorran took several blankets off the stack of supplies and spread them next to her. "You should get some sleep. You look tired." He motioned toward the pile of blankets.

Little wonder after all she'd been through in the past twenty-four hours. "I am exhausted," she admitted as she scooted over onto the blankets. "But I'm too wound up to sleep. Does that make sense?"

He nodded, lips curving in a tentative smile. "I've been there many times."

"I need to think of something other than Heather." She sighed. "Can we just talk for a while?"

"Of course." After an awkward pause, he pulled off his boots and joined her on the makeshift bed. "What would you like to talk about?"

She looked at him, struck again by his rugged good looks. He had a quiet intensity that smoldered, rather than blazed. He was controlled and disciplined, using only as much aggression as necessary. It was a trait many of the Outcasts lacked, and she found it surprisingly attractive. They stared at each other for a moment before she realized he was waiting for her to answer. "I know you haven't been with the Outcasts very long. What made you join?"

He tensed, his gaze shifting to the wall directly in front of him. "I was in the RPDF for the majority of my life. It's the only option for most battle born males."

"The RPDF?" Almost without thought, she reached over and buried her fingers in the cub's soft fur.

"Rodyte Planetary Defense Force. My homeworld's military. I was taught to follow orders without hesitation and to protect the chain of command. I was dedicated and loyal, even after most of my friends had joined the rebellion. I'd made a promise, took a vow. That meant something to me." Despite the devotion he described, pain shadowed his gaze.

"What happened?" It was obvious this wasn't where the story ended.

"Military life suited me and I quickly fulfilled most of my goals. My last position was first officer aboard the *Triumphant*. My commander was Apex General Bidon Paytor."

"Apex general? That sounds important." She ran her hand along the cub's back, soothed by the softness caressing her fingers.

"He commanded the entire Rodyte fleet and answered only to the planetary monarch." His deep tone was filled with pride and a soft sort of wistfulness.

"Okay, so you worked for the head honcho." She smiled. "Was he a good commander? Did you enjoy working for him?"

"I enjoyed being aboard the *Triumphant*. The ship was brand new and massive. It had capabilities that none of us had ever seen before." He didn't say any more for a long time, then added, "Paytor was...flawed. His pursuit of the rebels became an obsession he used to justify all sorts of rash and radical actions."

"I can see why that would make you want to leave, but why join the Outcasts rather than the battle born rebellion?"

"I betrayed Paytor, made it possible for the rebels to capture him and take possession of the *Triumphant*. Even though I'd helped the rebels, to most I was still a traitor, unworthy of trust."

She shook her head, absently stroking Wenny's back. "That doesn't make sense. If your actions benefited their cause, why wouldn't they trust you?"

He shook his head. "I betrayed my commander. What's to keep me from doing so again if the next enemy offers me more than the battle born have to give? Once a traitor, always a traitor."

She narrowed her gaze and studied him. Despite being an outlaw gang, the Outcasts were actually picky about who they invited to join their ranks. If the overlord invited Xorran, then his decision to betray Paytor had to be justified. "Why did you switch sides? There's usually a specific reason, a catalyst that motivates people to act. What was yours?"

"Paytor ordered me to assassinate someone. It wasn't a military offensive. It was coldblooded murder."

That made no sense at all. "You're a tracker, not an assassin. Why wouldn't he have sent someone like Torrin?"

"Long involved story that I'd rather not get into right—ever. I'm not that person anymore. Suffice it to say, my trust was misplaced and I'm thrilled to be parted from all of it."

"Can I ask one final question about your past? It will be the last one, I promise."

He sighed, long and loud, but said, "Sure."

"Power like yours must be controlled. How did you learn how to use your abilities?"

"I was less than a year out of training when a crewmember didn't report back in after a mission. His teammates insisted he hadn't been captured and he was still on the planet where the mission took place. I instinctively knew where he was but explaining how I knew meant admitting I was clairvoyant. I struggled with the decision for many hours, but finally told my commander. He was shocked yet intrigued by the revelation, so he told his commander." The story grew progressively more unpleasant after that, so he hesitated.

"What happened?"

"I was transferred to the science division and was ordered to allow whatever testing the doctors and scientists required.

At that point my empathy was unimpressive, but a male being born with any active ability was highly unusual."

"How long were you their guinea pig?"

"Four and a half years." He looked at her, gaze filled with shame. Then he looked away. "When understanding my abilities wasn't enough, they began augmenting them. It was even more horrendous than you can imagine, but it made me very powerful. Very useful."

She reached over and touched his arm, waiting until he looked at her to say, "Your people betrayed you long before you turned on Paytor. I'm glad you joined the Outcasts. Rodytes don't deserve you."

Something in her words, or tone, made him smile. "The decision was easy. I refused to trade one master for another. I wanted an entirely different sort of life, the sort the Outcasts are trying to build."

As the intensity of his confession faded, awareness returned. She felt the heat of his skin sink into her palm and the solid shape of his forearm beneath her fingers. She wanted to open his shirt and explore his amazing chest.

He raised his hand and stroked her cheek with the back of his knuckles. Then he slipped his hands under her arms and swung her toward him, bringing her across his lap, facing him. She quickly folded her legs to either side of his thighs and straddled his lap. He was so much taller than her that their eyes, and mouths, were nearly on a level. His hands settled on her hips, anchoring her in place without touching her any more intimately.

"Now you know what brought me here," he told her. "I know you're second guessing your decision, but why did you volunteer in the first place?"

Unable to resist her need to touch him, she placed her hands on his chest, then ran them up onto his broad shoulders. "My childhood and adolescence was a mostly pleasant sort of chaos. I had loving parents, but their generosity often spread them too thin, especially from the perspective of their children."

"I'm not sure what you mean." His already deep voice took on a whispery growl that sent shivers down her spine. He still wasn't touching her anywhere but her hips, yet the position was undeniably intimate. Restlessness set in, making it hard for her not to wiggle and rock, rub herself against him.

"I have three biological brothers, and there was a continual stream of other kids flowing in and out of our lives." Rather than wait for him to voice his confusion, she clarified, "My mom and dad were what's called foster parents. They took in children who had lost their parents, or whose parents were no longer taking care of them. Sometimes the foster kids would stay a few weeks. Sometimes they stayed several years. My parents were even willing to take on those with complicated medical issues, so the authorities took advantage of them."

"It is honorable to help those in need, but I also see how it would have compromised their time with you and your biological siblings."

"Mostly it was good for us. It taught us how to share and revealed how fortunate we were to have a loving family. So many had little or nothing. But I was the oldest, so a lot of the extra work fell on me. In a lot of ways I feel like I never had a childhood. I was a built-in babysitter and my parents had no problem taking advantage of the convenience."

"Having so many children in their lives was your parents' decision, not yours. It was unfair for them to force the responsibilities on you. That must have been horribly frustrating."

"It was. It also left me longing for something entirely my own. I know that sounds selfish, maybe even petty, but I never had my own bedroom. Most of my clothes were secondhand. We weren't poor, exactly. There were just so many places for the money to go, so many mouths to feed, and bodies to clothe. By the time I turned eighteen, I couldn't wait to leave."

He caught a lock of her long, dark hair and wrapped it around his finger. "How did you make your living once you left your parents' home?"

If he wanted to talk, why had he dragged her onto his lap? She wanted to kiss him and wrap her legs around his waist so she could rub against him. "I work at an animal hospital. My upbringing left me with a need to help others. I chose animals and their caregivers."

That seemed to surprise him. "Did Isolaund know this when she gave you the cub?"

She shook her head. "I told Arrista, but it was after we left Isolaund."

He leaned forward slowly and her heart thudded in anticipation, but he angled away from her face and whispered in her ear. "You didn't answer my original question. Why did you volunteer to mate with a rebel?"

Damn it. He was doing it on purpose, making her desperate for his kiss. Well, two could play that game! "I was getting there." She wiggled closer, lightly pressing her breasts against his chest as she pushed one hand into his hair. "Because I left home so early, all I'd ever been able to afford were the basic necessities, tiny apartment, old beat-up car. I never went anywhere fun or did anything exciting. And my romances were about as memorable as everything else in my life. The transformation program was a chance to experience something new and extraordinary. And completely *mine*."

A sexy smile slowly parted his lips and desire made his purple phitons shimmer. "None of that has changed. You just got a little more adventure than you expected. We want the same things, a partner in life, someone to share our hopes and dreams, maybe children someday. Do you really want to return to your boring existence on Earth?"

She thought about her shabby apartment and nonexistent social life. She liked her job, found it rewarding. But work was supposed to enrich her other interests, enable her to live life to the fullest. The problem was, she didn't have anything in her life but work.

One of his brawny arms wrapped around her waist and pulled her even closer. "You're already restless, so I suspect this is going to hit you hard. Don't be afraid of the intensity. I won't take advantage. I promise."

She found his words odd and arrogant, until his mouth locked onto hers.

Chapter Four

Sara tensed, uncertainty holding her hostage for one breathless heartbeat. Xorran's lips were warm and surprisingly gentle. He'd made contact with obvious intent, then backed off and leashed his aggressive impulses. As soon as she'd learned they were compatible, this had been inevitable. The pull only amplified attraction. If she wasn't attracted to him naturally, there would be no reaction to his pheromones. The trouble was, she knew damn well she was attracted to him. She liked his slow, secretive smile and quiet intensity, had already learned to depend on his strength. She felt safe with him, secure in a way she'd longed for all her life. Did she dare bring sexual hunger into the mix? Did she want to make herself that vulnerable?

He didn't give her long to debate. His lips caressed hers, tongue softly teasing until she opened, silently inviting him inside. Still, he advanced slowly, giving her plenty of time to pull away. His tongue gently pushed into her mouth, spreading his taste and mixing his breath with hers. She shivered, then moaned as tingling heat cascaded through her body. Her nipples peaked and her core clenched. The restlessness building inside her suddenly flared into focused desire.

She wrapped her arms around him, holding firmly to his muscular back. He angled his head, taking the kiss deeper.

Their tongues slid and curved, caressing as they learned the other's taste and texture. He tugged her shirt out from her pants and splayed his fingers across her bare skin. His hands were so large, he spanned her back. Still, she wasn't frightened by his size or strength. Rodyte males protected their females. Instinct and honor prevented them from doing anything that would harm...

And yet the Outcasts had kidnapped her, taken her from the only world she'd ever known. Was that not harmful? She had a family and friends that were doubtlessly worried about her. Surrendering to Xorran rewarded the Outcasts for their outrageous behavior. Stubborn resistance filled her heart. She'd be damned before she gave them what they wanted, what they'd taken without permission.

She eased her hands between their bodies and pushed against his chest. "No," she said firmly, but her voice shook, ruining the effect. "I will not be a slave to my body. I do not want this."

He lifted her off his lap and set her back on her side of the blankets. "No means no, even on alien planets." But a wily gleam in his eyes warned that the battle of wills was far from over. "Get some sleep. The construction crews will return shortly after dawn, which means we need to build some sort of enclosure before then."

Her pulse still raced and her mind whirled, but she nodded and lay down. She curled up on her side, back to him. They'd only kissed for a moment, so why was her skin still tingling? Her core ached, and her breasts felt heavy, the tips sensitized.

Closing her eyes, she willed away the pulsing need. *This isn't real. It's not natural.* The reminder did little to ease the cravings. She wanted him to lie down behind her and push her pants to her knees. Then he could ease his cock between her thighs and fill her core, make her shiver and moan as he rocked in and out of her body. He'd hold her tight as he claimed her, keep her safe and secure while they established a connection that would last a lifetime and beyond. She wanted it, needed it.

This was ridiculous! All he'd done was kiss her.

She heard him moving around and saw the light fade through her eyelids. She opened her eyes to a darkness broken only by thin hints of moonlight streaming through uneven boards. His body heat faded and she feared he'd moved away, perhaps even left the room. Turning her head sharply, she saw the outline of his big body behind her. He lay on his back, arms raised, hands tucked under his head. Every part of his body lay just out of reach.

"Is it this hard for you?" she whispered, resenting his apparent calm.

"Give me your hand and I'll let you feel for yourself." The challenge in his tone was tempered by a hint of humor.

Turning back around, she squeezed her eyes shut and concentrated on her breathing. This was how it started, how they gradually eroded the will of a rational female and turned her into a mindless slave. The melodramatic thought made her smile. Most of her cabin mates were now bonded, so Sara had watched the progression three different times. Jillian had been first. She was young and naive, so no one was surprised when she fell for one of the guards. But Lily was mature, logical, an independent career woman with no interest in a mate. So when she fell for Arton, the enigmatic harbinger, everyone was shocked. They weren't even genetically compatible, and still

Arton found a way to win Lily's heart. Then Thea accepted the claim of Rex, the charming smuggler who worked for the Outcasts, and Sara began to wonder if there was something about Rodyte males that was irresistible to human females. Thea was still grieving the loss of her family, and Sara had been sure nothing and no one would be able to penetrate the emotional walls she'd built around her heart. But Rex accomplished the impossible, and they both seemed thrilled with the result.

Sara sighed, struggling to find a comfortable position on the hard floor. This rambling review of past events wasn't helping her relax. Oblivion was the only escape she had from this hunger, yet the persistent ache was making it impossible to sleep.

"Talk to me," Xorran suggested. "Let's think about something other than the pull."

She didn't want to talk, she wanted to strip off her clothes and crawl on top of him. Instead, she swallowed hard and forced her vocal cords to work. "I can't think of a subject that doesn't involve sex."

He chuckled. "Then talk about sex. How old were you when you shared pleasure for the first time?"

A memory stirred, but it barely penetrated the sensations pulsing through her body. So much had happened since she left Earth. She didn't even feel like the same person any more. "There wasn't a lot of pleasure involved. Neither of us knew what the hell we were doing." After an awkward pause, she added, "I was seventeen."

"I beat you by a year, and my first time was equally disappointing."

"Well, you certainly know how to kiss," she whispered, shivering at the memory. "I presume you've acquired other skills over time."

"I'd be happy to demonstrate."

She smiled, but didn't feed his ego. "My second lover was very different from my first. His name was David. We were together for almost two years. I honestly thought it would last much longer."

"Why did the relationship end?"

There was a tension in his voice that hadn't been there before, so she chose her words carefully. "He finished his training and moved back home so he could open his own practice. Ended up marrying his childhood sweetheart. I was a college fling. I just didn't know it at the time."

"What sort of practice? Did you also attend this college?"

"David was training to be a veterinarian when I met him, and no, we didn't go to the same college. He went to a private university, while I got a certificate from a local trade school. That should have been my first clue that he wasn't taking me seriously. Trust fund snobs don't marry local riffraff. We're good enough to bone, but not to marry."

He placed his hand on her hip, but made no other move to touch her. Heat sank through her uniform pants, feeding the restlessness. "Many of those words are unfamiliar, but I recognize your tone. Battle born sons are frequently treated with derision and made to feel worthless. This man was not better than you just because he had wealth. You are kindhearted and ambitious, intelligent and beautiful. You have accomplished much despite the disadvantages of your upbringing. If I may borrow an Earth phrase, screw him."

She smiled, knowing he couldn't see her. Then she realized she hadn't really finished the story. "Anyway, David was doing a sort of residency at the animal hospital where I worked. When it was over, he went back to his 'real' life and left me behind."

"That must have hurt you deeply." After a long, silent pause, he asked, "Do you still have feelings for this male?"

"Not even a little. The end came without warning. He sent me an email explaining why he broke it off. The cowardly way he left made getting over him a whole lot easier. All I regret is the wasted years."

"I'm sorry he hurt you." He slid his hand up her side and touched her hair, just a hint of a caress, then he pulled away. "How many serious relationships have you entered into since?"

She immediately missed the hint of intimacy, the physical connection of his hand on her body. "David was as close as I ever got. After him, I decided romance wasn't worth the trouble and focused on my job. Animals are easier to love than most humans."

"Makes me glad I'm not one."

She laughed. "A human or an animal?"

"Either. Both. Though I'm feeling rather animalistic right now. You better keep talking."

His warning sent a ripple of heat passing through her body. He wasn't even touching her now. Maybe that was the problem. He scooted closer. She could feel his body heat along her back and down her legs, but he still didn't touch her.

"How long ago was the breakup?" he prompted.

"Almost four years."

"You haven't shared pleasure in four years?" He sounded incredulous. "Isn't that unusual for humans?"

"I didn't say I never had sex. I said I haven't bothered with a serious relationship. I don't sleep around, but I flirt, and sometimes that flirting leads to...sharing pleasure." Silence fell, making her feel awkward and alone. Was he angry? She knew Rodyte males could be territorial, but he'd asked her to talk about this. "What about you? How many females have you shared pleasure with? Have all your lovers been female?"

He suddenly rolled her onto her back. His gaze gleamed in the dimness, purple phitons starting to glow. "Are you mocking me?"

"No. You seem annoyed by my honesty. I thought it only fair that you reciprocate."

"I've had seven sexual partners, and yes they were all female." He slipped his arm beneath her neck and placed his other hand on her belly. "And I'm not annoyed. I'm jealous. Thinking of you with anyone else makes me want to inflict bodily harm."

"On me?" she gasped.

"Never! I will never harm you and anyone who tries to must come through me."

"Why?" His reaction seemed melodramatic, almost silly. "You barely know me."

"I know your scent and your taste. There is no doubt you are my mate, the one female with whom I am meant to spend the rest of my life."

"I'm a *potential* mate. That's very different. One is like winning the lottery. The other is like being handed a ticket for the lottery. There are still a lot of obstacles between you and the prize."

"Challenge accepted." His tone roughened and his fingers pressed into her flesh, not hurting, just making her more aware of his touch. "You are an incredible prize, so I will gladly undertake each task and navigate each obstacle."

He was so adorably serious that it made her smile. "Well, lover boy, the first obstacle is getting us both to sleep. Any suggestions?"

A wicked smile parted his lips, his teeth barely visible in the darkness. "Let me touch you, Sara. I'll make you come so many times you'll have no choice but to sleep."

She shivered and tingles branched out from her spine. "We *both* need to sleep. I'm pretty sure that won't make you sleepy."

He leaned down and kissed each corner of her mouth. "It would be well worth it."

She couldn't believe she was even considering it, but her body ached and it had been a very long time since she'd felt anything resembling passion. "Answer me honestly. Will this help or make the cravings worse?"

"I will never lie to you." He was so sincere it sounded like a vow. "The pull will subside for a time, but the urgency will return and continue to intensify until I claim you, or another male ignites a hunger even more demanding than this."

Her eyes widened and she stilled. "Is that even possible? I'm going insane right now."

He grinned, clearly pleased by her admission. "The pull's intensity is determined by the strength of our natural attraction. I find you extremely pleasing, so my need is nearly overwhelming."

There was no need for him to spell out that the same was true with her. She was experiencing the phenomenon right now. Still, each woman who gave in made it that much harder for the others to resist. Somehow the Outcasts had to be taught that their actions were dead wrong.

His gaze narrowed and tension returned to his voice. "What are you thinking about? I thought you didn't want a mate."

"I don't know what I want," she cried. "This is so unfair! I made a conscious decision to participate in a daring program back on Earth. It was risky and a little scary, but I was still in control. Instead, I was taken half a galaxy away from my home, my family and friends. The situations might be similar, but they are not the same."

"You're right." He rolled to his back and carefully withdrew his arm from beneath her neck. "You told me you're not willing to be courted. I shouldn't have kissed you."

She indulged in a humorless laugh, finding his reaction absurd. "It's a little late for regrets. That train already left the station."

Rolling back to his side, he propped his head on his hand. "What are you saying? Do you want me to touch you are not?"

"I want a lot of things all at once. How the hell am I supposed to decide?"

"You've already decided." He lightly touched the side of her face, his thumb brushing over her lips. "Speak the words. Tell me what you want."

She closed her eyes, hating these sorts of games. David loved making her beg. She'd always found it infuriating rather than sexy.

"It's not a power play, love. I need to know you're willing."

Relieved that she'd misunderstood, she opened her eyes and whispered, "Yes. God, yes. Touch me. I need your touch."

"Who am I?" The light in his eyes flared, the intensity demanding an answer.

My mate. The words popped uninvited into her mind. "Xorran," she said firmly, refusing to acknowledge the claim he was trying to establish. She still had serious doubts about allowing him to court her, but she couldn't think clearly about anything until the cravings subsided.

Slowly, he lowered his face, gaze boring into hers. Time paused, trapping her in the moment and narrowing reality to Xorran and her. His warm breath stirred against her lips, his scent slowly filling her nose. He was strong and handsome, smart and kind. And he offered security and a sense of belonging that she'd longed for all her life. Why was she so afraid of making the promise reality?

His lips pressed against her and she closed her eyes, blocking out thought and insecurity. He'd lit a fire in her body and now he was going to fan the flames until there was nothing left but ash. She only hoped that she would survive the inferno.

He pushed his arm back beneath her neck as his mouth caressed hers. As before, the kiss was slow and coaxing rather than harsh and demanding. He could be aggressive. No one rose through the ranks of any military without being ruthless, even lethal. But with her, he was gentle, patient.

Tired of denying her body what it needed so badly, she parted her lips and raised her hand to his face. Bristle roughened his jawline, but higher, along the crest of his cheekbone, his skin was warm and soft. She explored his shapes and textures while he traced her lips with the tip of his tongue. All the while their breaths mingled and mixed, making her head spin and her nipples tingle. Her heartbeat accelerated, amplifying the throb between her legs. She needed him there, filling the emptiness, stretching her core until she screamed with pleasure.

As if sensing her thoughts, his tongue pushed into her mouth, sliding along hers until his taste exploded along her taste buds, sending a fresh rush of desire all through her body. She groaned, hips canting, legs thrashing restlessly.

He slid his thumb along the collar of her uniform top, triggering the seam release. Cool air wafted across her breasts as he parted the sides, baring her to the waist. His hand soon followed, cupping, gently squeezing, and then teasing the nipples with the pad of his thumb or a careful pinch. She groaned into his mouth as darts of sensation zinged from the tips of her breasts to her clit. Desire rose, burning brighter as his skillful touch awakened her senses.

Eager to feel more of him, she drew his shirt from inside his pants. He wore the clingy pullover style many of the men favored. The fabric came free and quickly bunched below his arms. She tore her mouth away from his long enough to whisper, "Off." She tugged on the shirt, illustrating what she wanted. He tore the garment off, obliging her with nearly violent haste, then his mouth recaptured hers.

She stroked his chest and shoulders, lingering over his arms, fascinated by the bunch and flex of his impressive muscles. All the Outcasts were lean and fit. Some were even more handsome than Xorran. But he was hers, hers to touch and taste, talk to and depend on. If she allowed his claim, they would share thoughts and emotions. There would be no lies, no pretense or deception. But she had to be willing to give him the same access to her mind. She had to be brave enough to believe his promises, and risk her heart.

Something deep inside her shifted, she softened, opened, and not just physically. She wanted to make love to him desperately, but she wanted more, she wanted that deeper connection, the absolute intimacy only experienced by bonded mates.

She returned his kiss with greater fervor, arching into his touch. "Oh Xorran, I want—"

"I know, love. I know." He quickly unfastened her pants and slipped his hand inside, misunderstanding the nature of her longing. Then his fingers curved over her mound, pressing against her damp folds.

Urgent desire blazed through her abdomen, making her cry out. Rational thought was consumed in the flashfire as he gently parted her, and settled two fingers over her clit. With a few circular strokes he triggered her first orgasm. Pleasure pulsed through her core, rippling and clenching, which only made her feel empty and even more needful. She bucked helplessly, wanting him over her, *inside* her.

He peeled her pants down to her ankles then moved her legs apart. She didn't resist, was beyond modesty or shame. His long fingers pushed into her wet center and she whimpered. The slight penetration felt amazing, but it also teased, making her anxious for more.

"You're so wet," he muttered as he kissed his way down her neck.

"Sorry," she responded automatically, feeling a spark of embarrassment surrounded by burning need.

"I wasn't complaining." He looked down at her, eyes gleaming with predatory light. "It just makes me want to taste you."

Her only response was a helpless whimper as he lowered his mouth to one tight nipple, and then the other. She'd never thought of her nipples as particularly sensitive, but that strange string connecting them to her clit hadn't existed before. Each time he sucked on her breast, her clit twitched and tingled.

His hand moved between her thighs, sliding his fingers in and out of her wet core. She rocked her hips as she stroked her fingers through his hair, lost in the sensory maelstrom swirling around and through her. She came again with a sharp gasp, the burst of pleasure completely unexpected.

He kissed his way lower still and she squeezed her eyes shut. She knew what he intended. He hadn't been subtle about his ultimate destination. His fingers slowly withdrew and she fought back another whimper. They made her sound so helpless, so pathetic. Then he pulled off her boots and finished removing her pants. Her arms were still in the sleeves of her uniform, but her entire body was exposed and available. She opened her eyes just in time to watch him climb between her thighs and open her legs even farther.

"I should have turned the light back on before we started." He voice was a sexy growl in the darkness, and all she could see was the outline of his body and his eyes. "I want to savor this view."

Emboldened by the dimness, she arched her body, thrusting out her breasts and then raising her hips. "I thought you were hungry."

An actual growl rumbled and she tensed. Was the cub awake? But the sound came again half a second before Xorran's mouth covered her slit. No, the growl was definitely the male, not the cub. He shoved his tongue deep into her body, doubtlessly coating it with her cream. She gasped at the aggression, but loved the blatant carnality. It made her feel wild and free. He did it again and again, claiming her the only way she'd allow—at least for now.

He quickly worked her to another orgasm. Her inner muscles pulsed around his tongue as waves of pleasure swept over her. Then he drew back and gently sucked on her folds, licking every crease and furrow until she was squirming again. Only then did he settle his lips over her clit. She'd already come three times and still the need throbbed inside her, making her restless and desperate.

He teased her this time. Sucking gently, then pausing to gently lick the sensitive nub. Pleasure built gradually, coiling inside her like a giant spring. He parted her folds with his thumbs, holding her open so his lips could more easily fasten onto her clit. He was persistent and patient, two qualities that quickly drove her mad. She pushed up with her heels, pressing herself against his mouth. It did no good. He refused to be rushed. The urgency swelled, gathering tighter, and tighter. And then he backed off, refusing to let it crest.

"Enough!" she cried as he denied her for the sixth time. "Either let me come or let me up."

He pushed up on his elbow. "What's the matter, love? Doesn't that feel good?" He released her folds and stroked her with his thumb as he pushed his fingers deep into her aching core.

"You're killing me and you know it." She panted, bucking, driving herself onto his fingers. "Even this is a tease." A sob broke through her voice and she turned her face away. "I need you, all of you."

He moved back to her side while his hand continued to pump between her wide-spread thighs. "Squeeze me tight, and pretend that's my cock."

She sobbed again, feeling foolish even as she cried, "I don't want to pretend. I want you inside me."

"I know, baby. I know." He kissed her and thrust harder with his fingers, faster.

Shaking violently, she tightened her inner muscles, squeezing as hard as she could to maximize the fullness. His tongue took on the rhythm of his hand, filling her mouth as his fingers filled her core. She relaxed into the swelling need rather than fighting against it. She was confused and intoxicated. He was being selfless and responsible. He'd promised not to take advantage of her eagerness and he was true to his word. Despite feeling the cravings himself, he was protecting her from the pull.

The thought sent her over the edge. She arched clear off the blanket, crying out sharply into his mouth. Her body pulsed and surges of pleasure radiated through her abdomen, flowing down her arms and legs. She clenched her fists and curled her toes, riding the wave as far as it could carry her.

When reality returned he lay on his back beside her, staring up at the ceiling. She rolled to her side and curled up against him, resting her head on his shoulder. He spread a blanket over her nearly naked body as she gradually caught her breath. She didn't have the strength to move. She felt drained, replete. "What about you?" she whispered sleepily.

"You can make it up to me next time," he whispered back, then pressed a kiss into her hair.

Next time. The phrase made her smile as she closed her eyes and surrendered to sleep.

⟨ ⟩

WAKING WITH HIS MATE warm and naked in his arms made Xorran grin like a fool. He could still feel her arch into his caresses and hear the sweet cries of her pleasure. His balls ached and tension banded his gut, but he didn't care. He'd shared pleasure with his mate. Any lingering discomfort was a small price to pay.

He'd shared pleasure with his *potential* mate, his conscience reminded. Their courting had barely begun. Sara was still reluctant and afraid. And resentful that she'd been kidnapped. Still, last night gave him hope. Their natural attraction was clearly strong or the pull wouldn't be so overwhelming. She'd begged for him to take her. The night would have ended with him deep inside her if he were a less honorable man. A few moments of physical pleasure would never be enough. He wanted her willing. No, not just willing, he wanted her clear headed and excited about becoming his mate. If she didn't enter into this with equal enthusiasm, then what sort of life would they be able to build?

Kidnapping the females had been rash and reckless. He understood why the leaders had done it, but he never would have agreed had the decision been put to a vote. Abduction for any reason was wrong. His mother had been abducted and imprisoned. She'd been ruthlessly seduced and emotionally manipulated. He refused to follow in his father's footsteps! Starting off with a kidnapped bride was putting him at a distinct disadvantage.

Wenny raised her head, looked around as she yawned, then went back to sleep. Yesterday's trauma had clearly taken its toll on both females. Xorran put Sara's pants and boots right beside her so she could dress quickly should the need arise. He didn't want to wake her. She was sleeping so peacefully.

Slipping quietly from the room, he went outside and surveyed the area for possible enclosure locations. It needed to be near the Wheel, but not too near or the overlord would object. Xorran suspected as soon as word spread of a captive karron cub, Wenny would become a curiosity. He wasn't sure if the possibility was good or bad, but they needed to plan accordingly. Placing the enclosure between the Wheel and the barracks would provide the cub with continual supervision and protection once the barracks was occupied.

Blueish-green grass blanketed a relatively flat area. Xorran staked out the boundaries with the front half in the clearing and the back half in the trees. Until they had time to build some sort of house, the trees would offer shade from sunlight and shelter from inclement weather. A small stream would cut across the back corner of the habitat, offering Wenny a continual source of fresh water. They'd have to devise some sort of grate for the stream to ensure she couldn't swim out, but lugging water into the enclosure every day seemed foolish with the river nearby.

He was digging holes for fence posts when Sara joined him in the cool morning sunshine. A gentle breeze stirred the turquoise leaves on the surrounding trees and the briskly flowing water looked particularly green. Sara appeared fresh and rested, dark hair pulled back into a simple ponytail.

"Good morning." He paused in his task and wiped his sweaty face on his uniform top, which he'd removed again.

Her dark gaze swept over his torso as she responded, "Good morning. I like your outfit." She flashed a playful smile, then licked her lower lip. Was she thinking about their kisses and all the pleasure he'd given her.

"I knew it was your favorite. That's why I wore it."

Her smile broadened into a sexy grin. "Maybe tomorrow you can wear the shirt and not the pants."

His gaze narrowed as blood rushed to his groin, painfully hardening his cock. "Keep it up and I won't wait until tomorrow."

She raised both hands in surrender. "I'll behave."

"Is the cub still sleeping?" he asked after they stared at each other for a long hot moment.

She nodded, then cleared her throat. "How long have you been out here?"

"Not long. Did you sleep well?" he asked with a cocky grin. She'd snuggled against him all night. He knew damn well she'd slept like a baby.

She ignored the question and motioned toward the staked-out area. "This space will be fine for now, but she's growing really fast."

"This is temporary," he stressed. "Once we have more information about karrons, we'll choose a location for a permanent habitat."

Crossing her arms over her chest, she frowned. "I don't want her confined any longer than absolutely necessary. She needs to be returned to the wild."

The sentiment was compassionate yet naive. "If she's part of Isolaund's feline army, she was likely born in captivity. I'm not sure she'd know what to do in the wild."

She made a helpless gesture, then sighed. "It's impossible to make the best decisions for her with so little information."

"Agreed. We need to get a message to Arrista, maybe even a list of questions she can answer."

"Our only line of communications right now is Arton." Frustration was clear in her tone and expression. There wasn't much more that could be said about that subject, so her agile mind moved on. She motioned toward the holes he'd dug. "Where are we going to get fence posts? Or fencing, for that matter? The logs they're using for the barracks are huge."

"The ships can produce smaller items. It just requires a lot of energy."

"Of course. We use the nutria-gens all the time, but I forget about the other matter generators."

Xorran nodded. "The overlord wants to wean us off the nutria-gens too. This land can provide us with everything we need to thrive. We just need to learn how to process the resources."

Much to his surprise, Sara rolled up her sleeves and grabbed a shovel, working right alongside him for the next hour. She paused at one point and wiped her sweaty face with her sleeve. "I thought you were just showing off, but it's getting hot fast." She looked at him and flashed a flirtatious smile. "Should I take my shirt off too?"

"Not unless you want to cause a riot."

Her brows drew together and confusion narrowed her gaze until she heard the voices and tromping boots. The construction teams rounded the bend and came into view a few seconds later. Xorran quickly warned them not to open the door in the back of the structure, telling them there was an animal confined in there.

Most of the workers simply nodded, but Mardon, the team leader, walked up to Xorran and asked, "What sort of animal and why is it locked up in my work site."

"It's a karron cub," Sara told him. "And she's only there until we can finish her enclosure." She motioned to the holes they were digging.

He whistled and waved some of his workers over. "Help them. We're not going to trip over a yowling battle cat all day." The workers took the shovels from Xorran and Sara and continued digging deep, narrow holes.

As if to support Mardon's position, Wenny began to meow and growl, sounding pathetically forlorn.

"She hasn't been out of that room in hours," Sara pointed out. "She probably needs to, you know, water a tree."

Mardon's expression went from mildly annoyed to angry in a flash. "If that thing shits all over the storeroom, you're cleaning it up!"

"Understood." Xorran rushed toward the storeroom, grabbing a long length of rope off a pile of supplies. He quickly devised a crude harness and leash. The karron greeted them both with obvious enthusiasm, butting her head against their thighs and weaving in and out of their legs. Wenny allowed Xorran to put the harness on her, but she fought against the leash so hard Sara wasn't able to control her. Xorran was glad for his thick work gloves as Wenny tested him with each forward lunge. The cub was still relatively small, but her bursts of strength were explosive.

The workers watched with overt fascination as Xorran led the cat outside.

"She has to be hungry," Sara said. "I know I am."

Xorran cringed. He'd been so focused on the habitat that he'd forgotten about food. "Let's get her settled, then we'll take a quick break."

"Deal."

They let the cub tromp through the trees, pawing and sniffing everything she passed. She seemed more interested in her new environment than tending to her bodily functions, but nature soon reminded her why she was there.

"What do we do with her while we have breakfast?" Sara mused. "If we feed her first, she might settle down, but the construction guy doesn't want her in the storeroom."

Before Xorran could reply, Arton walked into view. He looked at the cub and said, "*Deztee*," in a clear, authoritative tone, then held up his right hand, palm out.

Wenny immediately sat and calmed, staring up at him as she waited for his next command.

He turned to Sara with a half-smile. "I dream shared with Isolaund last night and she taught me some commands you might find useful. *Deztee* means stop, and the hand gesture means silence."

"That's wonderful." Then her enthusiasm paused and she asked, "How is Heather? Have they agreed to the prisoner swap?"

"Not yet, but Isolaund insists that Heather is protected. She said, not only is Heather well hidden, the Guiding Council warned General Alonov not to touch her and even the general must obey the council."

Arton's assurance soothed Sara's fears somewhat, yet compassion and worry still clouded her expressive gaze.

Xorran automatically wrapped his arm around her shoulders and pulled her close against his side. "We'll get her back before anything else happens to her."

She looked up at him, then sighed. "What are they waiting for?"

"Isolaund was equally frustrated," Arton insisted. "She said it takes much too long for the Guiding Council to make any decision, but she stressed that Heather is safe."

Turning back to the harbinger, she nodded. "It doesn't appear that we have any choice but to wait. Will you please teach me the commands? Wenny hates the leash. She'll probably be easier to control without it."

"Of course," Arton dipped his head, then added, "My mate would like to join you for the midday meal. She will either entertain you in our quarters aboard the *Viper*, or she will bring food here. The choice is yours."

"Here would be better, and tell Lily I'm looking forward to it."

Chapter Five

A cool breeze brushed across Sara's face and she sighed, yet contentment hadn't produced the sound. She felt restless, homesick, and confused. Everything was strange here. Even the air smelled different. The sky was bluish green, teal—like Toxyn's hair. She shuddered, refusing to waste energy thinking about her obnoxious abductor. Surrounded by aliens and elves, she'd never felt so out of place.

And then there was Xorran.

"Are you all right," Lily asked as she gathered the remains of their meal and put everything back in the alloy crate she'd used to bring the food here. They sat on a thick blanket beside Wenny's completed enclosure. The workers had surrounded the area with eight-foot-high wire fencing complete with a gate, installed grates over each side of the stream, and even built Wenny a simple house before returning to their original assignments. The Outcasts had many faults, but no one could deny they were industrious and efficient.

"I'm conflicted," Sara admitted. Their conversation during lunch had been light and superficial. Knowing they both needed a break from the dramas surrounding them, they'd avoided darker, heavier subjects. Well, Lily was preparing to leave and Sara needed a sounding board. "I'd convinced myself I wanted to refuse all my matches, even the ones I liked. I was ready to stand on principle, like Thea taught us, to leave the Outcasts no option but to take us back to Earth."

"Then Xorran kissed you?" Lily's smile was patient and understanding. "I felt the same way. I thought I'd lead by example, show the other women how resistance was our only weapon. Then Jillian volunteered for the program and the vote came back in favor of cooperating. Arton stopped being so arrogant, and everything just unraveled from there."

"Xorran makes me want things I'd never thought I'd want, at least not here. He's sweet and attentive, and he seems to enjoy my sense of humor, but they *kidnapped* us." Sara sighed. "This is not what I signed up for. I didn't want to sacrifice my family and friends. With a battle born mate, I would have been close enough to visit my brothers, or at least talk to them. I have two nieces and a nephew. I don't want them to forget about me. Am I just supposed to shrug all that off for the chance at a happy marriage?"

"Oh, Sara, this is so much more than marriage," Lily said with a secret smile.

Sara stood and brushed off her pants, frustrated by the continual reminders of how wonderful life would be if she just bonded with one of the males. Doubtlessly the sex would be amazing. Last night had proven that wasn't an exaggeration. But the instant connection and lifelong happiness couldn't be real. Life, at least her life, never worked that way. "I understand it's different, maybe even better, with a Rodyte, but it doesn't matter. They took away our freedom when they brought us to this remote planet. We're isolated and completely dependent on them. That's not okay. If we don't give in to them, our only alternative is to live alone and watch everyone else revel in bonded bliss. No matter how good they are in bed, that's emotional manipulation. I won't stand for it."

Lily pushed to her feet, her expression filled with compassion. "Arton's father will take you home if that's what you really want."

Shocked by the statement, Sara searched Lily's vivid blue gaze. Was she serious? "What are you talking about?"

"The overlord is still debating when and how to tell everyone, but Kryton Lux has offered to take anyone home if they've interacted with at least three of their matches and still want to return to Earth. Apparently, you qualify."

The news was so unexpected that Sara felt dazed. It took her a moment to speak at all, then her mind filled with questions. "How long ago was this decided? Why hasn't there been an announcement? Everyone has a right to know, not just those who have turned down their suitors."

"I agree, but the overlord doesn't. He feels the females can't make an informed decision unless they hear both sides of the argument. He insists that all the remaining females consented to becoming a mate when they volunteered for the original program. He just changed the location."

Blood rushed through Sara's ears, pulsing with such force that she could hardly concentrate. She could go home, see her brothers, her mom, her friends? Family had always been important to her. She'd never been tight with her parents, but her brothers were a different story. Especially Timothy, the youngest. He was twenty-two and about to graduate from college, the first in their family to accomplish the feat. Sometimes it felt more like Tim was her son than her brother. She was that invested in his life.

But if she left now, the spark she felt for Xorran would fizzle out before it had a chance to burn. He was so different than she'd expected, so different than the guards, or even Arton. Most of the Outcasts were war-hardened and bleak. None of them remembered how to smile. Xorran's smile was slow and often filled with secrets, but he still allowed himself to feel joy.

Wenny's soft growl drew her attention to the fence. The cub stared up at her with big blue eyes, head tilted to one side. Shit. What the hell would she do with Wenny? She couldn't just walk away from the cub. She'd promised to protect and care for her.

A strange tingling erupted in her head and she heard Wenny's uncertain vocalization again. Only this time, the sound played inside her mind. Sara thought she'd imagined the sound, then she heard it again.

What the hell?

A rush of images flowed through her mind accompanied by distinct emotions. She saw herself through Wenny's eyes and felt curiosity and uncertainty. Then she saw Wenny clinging to Xorran's body, trembling with cold and fear.

The memories faded as more detailed and evocative images took their place. She saw Xorran's slow, sexy smile, heard his warm laughter. She remembered his mouth moving over hers, tongue sliding deep into her mouth. His hands touched and teased with such skill, and selfless determination that it seemed like a dream. She'd never come that easily or that often. And she suspected every time with him would be that intense.

The two sets of memories contrasted and clashed. The sexy set had come from her mind, but the first... She couldn't explain how those had happened. It was all very strange.

"It's not just sexual, is it?" Lily guessed as the silence lengthened. "You really like him."

Shaking away the disconcerting muddle, Sara nodded. "Xorran's not like the others. He's quiet, thoughtful, not in-your-face aggressive. He seems more, dare I say, human."

Lily smiled. "He'd probably consider it an insult, but I understand what you mean. Many of the Outcasts had to become aggressive and hard to survive."

"And many were born that way."

Lily didn't argue. "At least now you can honestly decide if you want to bond with Xorran or not because you have another option."

Sara laughed. "I have seventy-one other options."

Lily smiled. "That's not what I meant."

"I know, and thank you for telling me. It definitely gives me something to think about."

"And I'll keep working on Arton about some sort of announcement. I've said all along that all the women have a right to know."

"Are Arton and the overlord as close as everyone says?"

Lily nodded. "They've known each other forever and have been through a lot together. If not for Kage, I'm not sure Arton would still be with us." She waved away the past with a flick of her hand. "But that's all behind us now. We're all focused on the future, and you should be too."

"It's easier to focus on the future when you know what you want it to be," Sara grumbled.

"I know." Lily gave her a hug. "You'll figure it out. I have faith in you."

Sara laughed. "Glad someone does."

"Thanks for having lunch with me." Lily bent and picked up the crate. "It felt wonderful to leave the lab for an hour or so. We need to do it again soon."

After Lily left, Sara carefully let herself into the enclosure. Wenny greeted her with a friendly head butt and her usual figure eight around Sara's legs. "I missed you too, silly cat." She scratched behind Wenny's ears and allowed her to show her excitement for a moment, then said, "*Deztee.*" She did her best to mimic Arton's authoritative tone. Wenny immediately sat. Sara raised her hand, palm out, and Wenny stopped growling and watched Sara attentively. "Whoever said cats can't be trained?"

Arton had also taught Sara the command for 'lie down', 'return to me', 'advance', and 'follow'. He'd demonstrated each and Wenny obeyed without hesitation. Clearly, the cub was smart and eager to please.

Sara looked deep into her expressive blue eyes, wondering what sort of life the cat had lived in the Underground. Was being trained for battle any better than life in the labor pool? Both seemed pretty horrible to Sara.

The tingling in her temples reappeared. She kept her gaze fixed on the cub, convinced this wasn't imaginary. The same plaintive growl sounded inside her mind, and then she heard a faint, tentative voice ask, *Sentiata*? Sara froze. That was the Sarronti word for mother.

Her eyes widened. Had Wenny just communicated with her?

"Did you enjoy your conversation with Lily?"

Her head snapped to the right and she found Xorran closing the gate behind him. He'd left when Lily arrived, but apparently hadn't gone far.

"I think she's telepathic," she told him, thrilled, yet still uncertain of the discovery. "Twice now, she's tried to communicate with me."

His brow furrowed as doubt narrowed his gaze. "What did she say?"

"The Sarronti word for mother. I'm not sure if she was calling me mother or asking where her mother is."

He smoothed his expression, but she still heard disbelief in his tone. "Did you try to respond?"

Refusing to react to his doubt, she bent to one knee and looked in Wenny's eyes. "What are you trying to say, baby. I don't understand."

Wenny's head tilted one way, and then the other, unblinking eyes staring back at Sara.

"She doesn't understand English." She unfolded her legs with a heavy sigh. "We need Torrin. He could talk to her in Sarronti."

Xorran frowned, obviously annoyed by the suggestion. "You should have him teach you how to do the loop thing with your translator so we can stop bothering him."

She agreed, but knew his concern had nothing to do with monopolizing Torrin's time. "Can you contact him, please?"

"Already did. He's on his way."

She nodded, anticipation starting to gather inside her. If they could talk to the cub, and if she could actually respond, that would change everything. The information they'd hoped to gather from Alonov's son might be accessible in the karron.

"I wonder if there's a command for go home? Isolaund was worried that Wenny would turn up back in the Underground because Wenny knows how to get there."

Xorran glanced at Wenny, then shook his head. "If there's an actual command, Isolaund will never tell us."

Sara agreed, though a command might not be necessary if she could ask Wenny questions. "I know how to find the approximate area where Arrista and I emerged. Do you think Wenny would point out the actual entrance if we took her there?"

He walked across the grassy clearing and stroked Wenny's head, studying her as he milled over the possibilities. "It's certainly worth a try, but we'll have to be careful. Didn't you say she'll be in danger if she returns to the Underground?"

"I did, and she will." Sara looked at the cub. Wenny watched them trustingly. Sara didn't want to put her in danger, but this might be their only chance to find the underground fortress. "We have to find a better harness than the rope. She didn't like that at all."

He chuckled. "I'm not sure she'll like this any better, but I had the same thought." He walked back to the gate and picked up a wad of what looked like leather straps. "I went and saw the programmer who designs our weapon belts and other accessories. He can print almost anything your imagination can conceive." He unwound the bundle and showed her the new harness and leash. It was sleek yet strong. The straps would circle Wenny's chest and upper legs rather than her neck, allowing her handler to guide her without fear of choking the cub. "The reinforced handle will make it easier to hang on and decrease the chances of being dragged."

"The new commands will help too," she reminded. "If she gets rambunctious, I know how to calm her down."

"Shall we give it a try?"

She nodded. "We can leave right after Torrin speaks with Wenny. I know Isolaund thinks she can protect Heather from Alonov, but I saw the look in his eyes. He will find a way to have her if we don't get her out of there. And the fear I saw on Heather's face." She shivered as compassion and anger combined to shake her composure. "I'll never get that image out of my mind. Heather is counting on me to save her. I can't let her down."

Xorran placed his hands on her shoulders and waited until she looked at him to speak. "This is a shot in the dark. We could get lucky. I hope we do, but it's more likely that this will fail. You must be realistic or I won't even attempt this."

Her chin raised and she squared her shoulders. "If we head into this thinking it's pointless, it will be pointless. I've always found optimism more helpful than being realistic."

"Fair enough," he relented with a smile. "We'll try it your way."

Wenny allowed them to strap her into the chest harness, but as before, she resisted the leash, desperately wanting to choose her own direction. Sara found the stubbornness endearing, yet corrected her with firm commands whenever she veered off course. They had the cub moving around the enclosure at a manageable lope when Torrin arrived.

"Did you capture another elf?" he asked, one hand grasping the alloy fence. His apparent cheer did little to disguise the lethal intensity lurking behind his gray-green eyes.

Hearing an unfamiliar voice, Wenny lunged forward, growling fiercely. "Easy, girl. He's a friend."

When the cub didn't react to Xorran's reassurance, Sara said, "*Deztee.*"

"Where did this little monster come from?" Torrin asked as he let himself into the enclosure. Despite the derogatory term, his tone was friendly, almost playful. He walked right up to Wenny and introduced himself in Sarronti. "Hey there, little monster. I'm Torrin and you're adorable." He bent to one knee and the cub approached, though a bit hesitantly. He held out his hand and the cub licked it, her way of saying hello.

Sara watched the exchange, shocked by the assassin's softer side. Had he known Wenny was telepathic or would he have tried to converse with any animal?

Female name? Wenny shifted her gaze from Torrin to Sara and back.

Sara was still processing the shock of hearing Wenny's mind voice again when Torrin replied in Sarronti. "Her name is Sara."

Holy crap. He could hear the cub too. She looked at Xorran. "Did you hear her question?"

Xorran shook his head.

Sara save me.

"Did she now?" Torrin stroked Wenny's head. "What did Sara save you from?"

The cub's head dropped and she made a soft, mournful sound. *Bad Wenny. Fail test.*

Torrin looked at Sara, confusion clear in his expression. "Do you know what that means?" He effortlessly switched between the two languages.

"Yeah, but it's not true. She did nothing wrong. Tell her the rules are bad not Wenny."

He repeated what she'd said in Sarronti and Wenny cautiously lifted her head. *Master send Wenny away. Must be bad.*

Desperately wishing she could speak directly to the cub, Sara knelt in front of her and took her furry face between her hands. "Mistress Isolaund was protecting you. She wanted you to be safe. Bad people are looking for you, so Mistress Isolaund asked me to take care of you until it's safe for you to return." She knew that day would never come, but the cub was clearly upset and frightened already.

Torrin translated.

It took the cub a few minutes to absorb what she'd been told, then she asked, *How long?*

"I don't know, sweetheart. But you're safe here. We won't let anything bad happen to you."

Bad already happen. Wenny alone. Apparently finished with the conversation, the cub lay down and rested her chin on her paws.

Sara sighed. She didn't know how karrons behaved in the wild, but she was pretty sure Wenny had been surrounded by other karrons her entire life. Well, there was nothing she could do about Wenny's loneliness right now. Heather had to take priority.

Shifting her gaze to Torrin, Sara asked, "How long would it take you to teach me how to speak Sarronti?"

He shrugged. "The technique is simple, but I have no idea how long it will take you to master it. Humans aren't used to manipulating energy."

"Can we at least try?"

"Of course." He took a step toward Sara, then paused and looked at Xorran. "I'll try to talk her through it, but I might need to touch her again."

"Understood," Xorran grumbled, arms crossed over his chest. Wenny's leash was still looped around his wrist though there was plenty of slack in the long synth-leather strap.

He had yet to act on his jealous instincts, so Sara let his attitude slide. She'd always steered clear of possessive men, found the characteristic often led to violence. Xorran was clearly possessive, yet he seemed focused on her safety rather than some deep-seated insecurity that he couldn't trust her. She wanted to learn more about him before she decided if it was a problem or not.

Torrin stood in front of her, within reach, but his arms remained at his sides. "Let's start with the basics. Could you feel it when I entered your mind?"

"Definitely." Torrin felt like a force of nature. She couldn't imagine anyone not realizing he was there.

"Good. Then follow with your mind. I'm going to lead you to the nanites."

"Okay." She sounded as uncertain as she felt. He might think this was simple, but it was surreal for her. He entered gradually. Not only could she sense his energy, she could sense the care with which he worked. The narrow stream wound and dipped, flowing like water, or blood. Then he stopped and tingles burst deep inside her mind.

"Can you feel that pulse?"

"Yes." She closed her eyes, concentrated, tuning everything out but Torrin's voice and the pulses of energy.

"I'm going to switch to Sarronti so you can feel the translator working. Memorize the sensations, the direction of the energy, the speed with which it flows."

She nodded.

"Ignore my words. Focus on the nanites. Try to see them if you can."

She pictured tiny fireworks, miniature bursts of silver and gold. He continued to speak, but she wasn't listening. His energy meshed with hers, then drew her closer to the translator. He flowed through the microscopic circuitry, guiding her, teaching her. He demonstrated how the devise worked, and how she could control it. After she'd followed him through several rotations, he paused.

"Say 'have a nice day,'" he coached.

"Have a nice day," she said in English.

He captured the pulse and looped it through the translator. The phrase repeated in Sarronti. The words weren't audible, yet she heard them clearly in her mind. "*Lartice san esfarno.*" Her eyes flew open as she spoke the words aloud, then gave a happy cry. "I did it." She looked at her teacher, his stern expression curbing her enthusiasm. "Was that right?"

"You tell me, but try it without me this time."

It was awkward and took much more concentration, but she finally heard the Sarronti phrase and repeated it aloud. "I was almost right. Have a nice day is *lartice sin esf marono.*"

"Much better." Torrin finally smiled. "Now all it will take is practice. But remember practice doesn't make perfect. Perfect practice makes perfect, so check your accuracy until it becomes more natural." He stepped back and motioned toward the cat.

"Are you trying to tame the karron, and does the overlord know she's here?"

"The overlord knows and the cub is the reason the elves let Sara go," Torrin told him.

Confusion still clouded his gaze, but he didn't ask for clarification. Instead, he turned to Sara and asked, "Did you need anything else?"

"No. You've been extremely helpful. Thanks again."

He dipped his head with a faint smile, then departed.

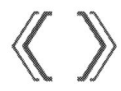

《 》

XORRAN WATCHED THE assassin until the forest swallowed his tall form. He hated that Sara kept turning to Torrin for assistance. He wanted to provide for all her needs, and ensure she was happy. Being this focused on another person was so strange. He'd always been concerned about his fellow soldiers, and then the males under his command. This was different, infinitely more intense. He wanted Sara to trust him and turn to him whenever she needed anything. It was physically painful to stand aside and let another male assist her.

She knelt in front of Wenny and spoke in stilting Sarronti. The cat didn't speak out loud, but apparently both Sara and Torrin were able to hear the cub's thoughts. After numerous exchanges, Sara stood and brushed off her knees.

"I didn't think humans were telepathic," he grumbled. Was he really jealous of a cat?

"I'm not. This has never happened before."

"Then how are you doing it?"

"I'm not doing anything," she insisted. "Wenny must have created some sort of link."

He accepted the explanation with a thoughtful nod. "Will she show us one of the entrances?"

Sara placed her index finger over her lips and shook her head. "We'll be right back," she told the cat, then led him from the enclosure. They walked well out of earshot before Sara stopped again. "She's remarkably intelligent, but she's also leery of us. I said one negative thing about Isolaund and Wenny's responses became very guarded, almost hostile. She's upset that she was sent away, and she is still loyal to 'the master.'"

"Damn."

"Oh, I haven't given up," she insisted. "I hate to trick her, but I don't see any other way. We'll pretend we received word from Isolaund that it's safe for Wenny to return to the Underground. Then we'll take her to the area of the forest where I emerged with Arrista. Hopefully, Wenny will get excited about going home and do the rest."

"And I'll pray she doesn't rip us to shreds when she realizes she's not going home and we tricked her."

She stilled, concern filling her expressive eyes. "I hadn't thought of that."

He considered the options for a moment, then said, "Let's check with Dr. Foran, see if he can give us some sort of fast-acting sedative to use if things get ugly."

"That's probably wise. If Wenny is anything like a human child, we could be in for a world-class tantrum."

Sara looked back toward the enclosure. "Maybe I should stay with her while you go—"

"Not a chance. She's safely confined and the construction site is teeming with workers. You're not staying here without me."

She smiled and color spread across her cheeks. "My striptease in front of the warlord was an exception not the rule."

He returned her smile, warmed by the memory. She'd been fiercely protective last night, like a mother guarding her young. And seeing her calves and lower thighs simply made him eager to see the rest of her supple body. "I only have your word on that, now don't I?" He moved closer, needing to touch her.

"My word should be good enough." She lifted her chin and playfully glared at him. "I'll never consider the claim of someone who doesn't trust me."

"Trust must be earned," he said sternly, thoroughly enjoying their game. "And you've been very naughty."

"Is that right?" Her brows arched and she placed her hands on his chest. "What's your strategy for reforming my behavior?"

His heart leapt at her touch and desire stirred inside him, rapidly building to a demanding roar. "I could lock you in my cabin. That will keep you out of mischief."

She grinned. "Thea and I caused all sorts of mischief when the overlord locked us inside a cabin."

"His mistake was leaving you together."

She laughed. "His mistake was leaving us unguarded."

"A mistake I'll be sure to avoid. In fact, the only way to ensure your appropriate behavior is if I guard you myself."

Challenge arched her brows even more dramatically. "You think you can handle me?"

"I'd sure as hells like to try." He leaned down and cupped her ass with both hands, easily lifting her off her feet.

She gasped, then laughed as she wrapped her legs around his hips. "I didn't realize you were an exhibitionist." She loosely circled his neck with her arms. "This should be fun."

Her gaze locked with his and her smile never wavered, so the importance of her words took a moment to sink in. *Exhibitionist?* He wasn't even sure what that meant. Then he looked to his left and groaned. The workers had all stopped and were watching them with lustful fascination. Did they honestly expect him to strip her naked and claim her right there in the grass? Well, if they hadn't had an audience...

Instead, he squeezed her butt and nipped her jaw. "We better take this somewhere a little more private."

"Why?" she whispered. "I'm not shy."

Desire exploded through his body as he imagined her wild and uninhibited, so lost in passion that she didn't care who was watching. She didn't pull away as he lowered his head, so he sealed his mouth over hers and filled his lungs with her scent. Her lips parted beneath his and her tongue boldly sought out his. They kissed and kissed until his knees threatened to give out and he had no choice but to come up for air.

"Dr. Foran," she panted, when he tried to capture her lips again.

"What about him?" Xorran supported her with one arm and fisted the back of her hair, slowly pulling her head back until their gazes locked.

"We need to go see if he has a sedative that will be safe to use on Wenny." Her breath puffed across his lips and her legs still clung to his sides.

Gradually, the world came back into focus. Sara was right. They couldn't do this right now. Heather was still in danger and Sara had no intention of resting until she knew her friend was safe. Accepting the inevitable, he reluctantly slid her down his body and set her feet on the ground. His aroused body protested loudly as he stepped back. "Shall we?" He swept his arm toward the path leading to the Wheel.

A collective groan erupted at the construction site, and Xorran remembered their audience.

Sara waved and blew them kisses, then called out, "Get back to work or I'll sic my battle cat on you!"

Laughter rumbled through the workers, then they turned and resumed their tasks.

Xorran and Sara walked for a moment in silence. He fought for composure, but he wasn't sure what occupied her mind. She seemed agitated though he couldn't name the cause.

"Are you all right?" he finally asked as they neared the Wheel. "You seem distracted."

She glanced at him, then stopped walking and met his gaze. "You're not what I expected. My other suitors were very different from you."

He searched her expression, trying to understand her emotions. She seemed controlled, even guarded right now. It was hard to believe this was the same woman who had kissed him so passionately a few minutes before. Of course, it hadn't taken him long to figure out her sarcasm and humor were tools she used to keep anyone from getting too close. He'd only sensed her emotions a couple of times, and each had been while she was extremely upset. "Is that good or bad?"

"Good for you, and I haven't decided for me."

She sounded sincere, but her answer seemed needlessly vague. With everything that was going on, he was tempted to leave it alone, give her the space she appeared to need. Yet she'd stopped walking as she brought up the subject, so it was obviously important to her. "How am I different?"

She started to speak, then sighed and looked away. "I don't know how to say this without insulting you."

"Just say it. I'm pretty hard to offend." Ordinarily, he wouldn't give a damn what anyone thought about him. But Sara was no random female. He wanted her as his mate, which made her opinion of him crucial.

"You don't seem as obsessed with all this as the others. You didn't even care enough about finding a mate to see how many females you matched. That part really bugs me. Do you even want a mate, or do you feel obligated to court me because we're compatible, and that's what the Outcasts expect of you?"

He caught her wrist and drew her into the trees beside the path. "After last night, can you really doubt how much I want you?"

"I know you want to have sex with me. That's not what I'm asking. Do you want to share your life with another person? Are you ready to commit to me for the rest of your life, never touch another female? Do you want children?"

He placed his hands on her shoulders, wishing they were alone instead of two steps away from a busy trail. "Most battle born soldiers don't dare to dream of such things. They are unattainable to us. The rebellion changed that, gave us license to dream. But I'm..." He lowered his arms and shifted his gaze beyond her. "I've been at the mercy of others for so long that this still doesn't feel quite real."

She nodded and the tension melted from her shoulders. "I've been there. Actually, I'm still there."

He met her gaze again and gently took her hand. "I don't want to give you the wrong impression, Sara. This might have come out of nowhere for me, but I'm thrilled by the opportunity. And the answer to all of your questions is yes. Yes, I desperately want a mate. Yes, I'm more than ready to commit to you. And yes, I want as many children as you're willing to give me."

Her only response was a smile as she pulled him back onto the path. Soon they headed up the ramp leading to deck one of the *Viper*. The commons was unusually crowded and it was clear from the excited buzz of overlapping conversations that something important was about to happen.

Sara paused near one of the other females and asked, "What's going on?"

The female, a rosy-cheeked blonde, responded, "There's supposed to be some big announcement."

All the ships were integrated now, so the overlord could easily send his signal to every display on all twelve ships. Humans seemed to band together whenever they faced uncertainty, so maybe this gathering was to be expected.

Their exchange seemed to be over, so he started across the room.

"Wait. I want to hear this," she objected.

"If it's important, the announcement will be transmitted throughout the Wheel. There's no need to wait around."

Her steps still dragged, but she continued walking.

They'd just reached deck two when the transmission began. The overlord's face filled every surface capable of producing an image. Xorran stopped and faced the display inset in the corridor wall. Sara stood beside him, tense and silent.

Kage had styled his hair, creating a tall, stiff ridge down the center while leaving the sides bare. The effect was most dramatic when paired with his barbarian-inspired garments. Today, however, he wore a khaki uniform, just like everyone else.

"Gossip pisses me off," he began without preamble. "Though peppered with elements of truth, it's ever-changing and never accurate. So, I thought I'd take a minute and set the record straight. As you've likely heard, we are not alone on this planet. We've encountered a race of beings known as the Sarronti. We know they visited Earth, so it's likely they're responsible for your mythological elves. We know very little about them, but we're actively working to learn more. For obvious reasons, they consider us a threat. It is not my intention to start a war. However, we will defend ourselves." He went on to explain about the kidnapping and the captured elf, as well as most of what Sara had told him.

"Do you realize how much of this he knows because of me?" Sara whispered as the overlord rambled on.

Xorran looked at her and smiled. "I'm proud of you and so is the overlord. You showed remarkable bravery in the face of terrifying danger."

She met his gaze for a moment before returning her attention to the display. "I wasn't fishing for compliments. It still seems like a bad dream."

He reached over and slipped his arm around her shoulders. "You're safe now and we'll get Heather back very soon."

"One last thing," the overlord was saying. "I've debated long and hard nabout this decision, but I feel it's time." He squared his already broad shoulders and import roughened his voice. "Any female who has interacted with at least three of her potential mates and still wishes to return to Earth will be allowed to leave. Retired General Kryton Lux has agreed to facilitate transportation. I fervently hope every one of you will decide to stay, but the decision is yours."

The image blinked off, but Xorran just stood there. Was the overlord serious? Without the females this place was just another mercenary outpost. "Did you know about this?" he asked Sara.

She nodded. "Lily told me at lunch."

The tension in her tone dropped a rock into the pit of his stomach. "Are you considering it? How many suitors did you refuse before you met me?"

"Four."

"Then you qualify for this...ride home. Are you planning to leave?" His heart lodged so firmly in his throat that he barely got the words out.

She shook her head. "Not right now anyway." A smile tugged at one corner of her mouth. "I can't leave Wenny."

"Is Wenny the only thing keeping you here?" If she wasn't serious about this, he'd rather know now. It wouldn't make her rejection any easier to bear, but at least it would be over quickly.

"I really like you, Xorran, and I didn't think I would." She took a deep breath and paused to lick her lips. "That's why I'm being completely honest with you. Being kidnapped is making this decision much harder than it would have been on Earth. I love the idea of having a mate, and children are something I've always wanted. But I'm not sure I can sacrifice all the other people in my life so I can build a future with you."

"You don't have to choose one or the other," he insisted. "I have access to spaceships. I can take you home to see your family. And the ban on off-world communications was to keep the battle born from finding out our location. If we're not hiding anymore, I can arrange for you to speak with anyone you like. I'll get clearance to make the call right now if that will make you happy." He took a deep breath and backed off. He was starting to sound desperate and that wouldn't help his cause. He had to earn her trust, not guilt her into feeling sorry for him.

"I won't lie to you. I simply don't know what I want right now."

"I understand." He cleared his throat and motioned down the corridor, but his heart was beating so fast he feared he'd pass out. "Main medical is that way."

With a sigh, she fell in step beside him.

As usual, main medical was busy. It took several minutes before Dr. Foran was able to speak with them, so they waited in his tiny office. Not only was Dr. Foran responsible for overseeing the other clinics in the Wheel, he ran the transformation program, with a strong assist by Lily. Xorran didn't know him well, but the doctor was surprisingly likeable, considering that he was a doctor.

"What a night," Foran said as he joined them in the office. He sank into the seat near his access station. "Speak very slowly so this lasts as long as possible. I'm exhausted." His hair was a lighter brown than a Rodyte's, and his strange green-gold eyes looked almost human.

"We need a safe way to sedate a battle cat cub if and when we lose control of her," Sara explained.

"How large is this cub?"

"Between fifteen and twenty pounds," Sara said.

"It needs to be a dart or something similar," Xorran warned. "If the cub goes off, it won't be safe to be near her."

"Understood." He pinched the bridge of his nose, then rubbed his eyes. "I have several medications that are used on Earth's big cats. I've never treated a karron before, but I've acquired quite a sampling of other animals from this planet and most are very similar to Earth's fauna. Anything we try will be experimental. However, my primary choice is frequently used by veterinarians on multiple worlds because it's tolerated well by a wide variety of animals."

Sara looked at Xorran, concern clear in her gaze. "Maybe we should just—"

"We're not even going to attempt this unless we have a way to interrupt a temper tantrum. She's scared and still very young. That's a dangerous combination."

"I know, but he said *experimental*. I don't want to do anything that could hurt her."

Dr. Foran reached out and carefully patted her hand. "I'll do everything in my power to minimize the risk, but I agree with Xorran. Karrons are predators. They're unpredictable. You cannot expect them to behave well all the time."

With a heavy sigh, Sara gave in. "I guess I don't have a choice but to trust you. How long will it take to synthesize?"

"I have the drug in stock. The problem is delivery. Prisoners are sometimes darted, but I don't think we have anything like that aboard any of the ships in the Wheel. Let me make some coms. If I can't locate a dart gun, I'll have my programmer print one." Foran scratched his chin and sighed. "This could take some time."

"Are you talking hours or days?" Xorran asked.

"Hopefully hours. Worst case scenario, tomorrow afternoon."

"Thank you," Sara said, though she was clearly disappointed with the outcome.

Dr. Foran just nodded, then returned to the chaos that was main medical.

"Two or three hours," Xorran muttered as they left the clinic. "However will we kill that much time?" He looked at her and allowed desire to ignite in his gaze.

"Actually, I'm kind of hungry." She batted her eyes in mock innocence.

He chuckled as he threaded his fingers through hers. "My thoughts exactly."

Chapter Six

They were already in each other's arms when the door to Xorran's cabin slid closed.

"We shouldn't do this," Sara whispered in between feverish kisses. Her doubts were still real, but her body didn't seem to care. All their teasing touches and hungry stares—not to mention the close call in the storeroom—had made this almost inevitable. And she was as guilty as he. She was finished pretending she didn't want him. It was pointless and dishonest. Still... "I'm not ready to be claimed." She pushed on his chest hard enough to get his attention.

He loosened his grip and eased back without letting her go. "I won't claim you until you want this as much as I do." His phitons glowed with amethyst fire and need hardened his features. "Let me show you what I'm offering. How can you choose if you don't really understand?"

That made sense. Or was it just an excuse for having sex with him? "I thought the link was permanent."

"A soul bond is. I'm talking about a transfer link. We could share emotions, even memories, but the connection can be dissolved."

He was easily the most attractive male she'd ever encountered, and it wasn't just his looks. He was strong and protective, without being a possessive jerk. They'd talked for hours without feeling awkward. If what he told her was true, he was everything she'd hoped for in a mate and then some. So why were they still talking? "This isn't a trick, a way to—"

"I would *never* take advantage of you like that." He tensed, lowering his arms. "Even to wonder about it questions my honor. I will protect you with my life. I will do nothing to cause you harm, ever!"

Rather than apologize for insulting him, she rolled up onto her toes and drew his head down to hers. Their mouths fit together, lips caressing as they gradually parted. He swept her up into his arms, then he took control of the kiss. She looped her arms around his neck, happily following his lead. He took a step then stopped, apparently lost in the kiss. Their lips clung while their tongues slid and curled, moving from her mouth to his and back.

When they were both breathless and needy, he started walking again. He broke away briefly and she looked around, noticing her surroundings for the first time. His cabin was at least twice the size of hers, and she had to share the space with others. His bedroom was separate from the main living area, and there was only one bunk, though it was wide enough for two.

"Officer perks?" she asked with an upraised brow.

He smiled. "There are no 'officers' among the Outcasts. The overlord assigned me this cabin because of my need for meditation and my ability to assist others."

"You meditate? When and why?" She knew so little about him. Everything he shared was another piece to the Xorran puzzle. She was eager to know more.

"Most mornings and any time I can't afford to be distracted. Tracking requires enormous concentration." He set her down beside the bed and reached immediately for the seam release tucked inside her collar.

She pushed his hand away and motioned toward his uniform. "You've already seen me. I want to see you."

He started to protest, then shrugged. "As my lady commands," he grumbled, bending to tug off his boots.

Following his example, she toed off her shoes as she asked, "Have you ever tracked down someone who was in real trouble?"

"Like Heather?" Shame and frustration sparked within his dark gaze.

"She doesn't count because elves are involved. I'm convinced they can do magic."

"Advanced technology is often mistaken for magic," he reminded as he took off his shirt. "We have shields that render our ships undetectable. Some can even appear to be other ships. I think the Sarronti are using a similar technology to mask the entrances to their lair."

She wiggled out of her pants and opened the front of her uniform top, but didn't take it off. "Can you track objects or just people?"

"I'm much more accurate with people, but I can do both." He stepped out of his pants and stood before her naked, clearly unashamed of his body. But then why would he be? He was lean and muscular from head to toe. "Why all the questions?"

Her appreciative gaze swept the length of his impressive form, lingering on the most interesting areas before returning to his face. "I want to know you before I sleep with you."

He moved closer, his gaze intense and bright. "Forming a transfer link will reveal me more completely than all the conversation in the universe. My answers could be lies, or exaggerations. The link will allow you to find the answers for yourself."

"And you'll be able to look into my mind too?" Did she want that? She didn't have any deep, dark secrets, but he'd feel how close she was to giving in. Could she trust him not to exploit the fact? "I'm not sure I'm ready for that."

He sighed, but his voice remained patient. "I can scan your mind whenever I like. I choose not to because I want to earn your trust. If you don't want me in your mind, that's all you need to say."

She would never know if she could trust him until she gave him a chance to prove himself. He'd been nothing but helpful and protective so far. Besides, what did she have to lose?

After a quick pause, she decided, "I have nothing to hide. I already told you my concerns." To make sure he understood, she shrugged out of the shirt and placed her hands on his chest. All she'd meant to do was demonstrate her surrender, but an electric pulse arced between them. Her fingers tingled and heat cascaded through her body, magnifying the ache between her thighs. She slid her hands up to his shoulders, then slowly ran them down his arms, pausing to explore the dramatically contoured muscles along the way. "Your body is sinful," she whispered.

His only response was a throaty chuckle as he tried to pull her closer.

"Not yet." She looked at him and added, "Please. Last night was your turn. Now it's mine."

He raised his hands in surrender, then lowered his arms and just stood there, letting her touch him.

She ran her hands eagerly over every inch of his well-toned body, avoiding his sex until she'd explored everywhere else. She knew all the Outcasts were like this, muscular and tall. They were mercenaries, and war required strength and endurance. But Xorran was hers, hers to touch however she liked, hers to bond with and love. If she could ever decide being mated was what she wanted. The temptation had never been so inviting.

She swallowed hard and finally wrapped her fingers around his cock. Like the rest of him, his shaft was long and hard. She stroked him from base to tip, fascinated by the contrast of soft skin over rock-hard flesh. "I want to taste you." Without waiting for his reply, she sank to her knees and guided him to her mouth.

A harsh groan escaped his throat as she took him deeper and deeper. He pushed his fingers into her hair, but didn't try to control her. She needed to learn his taste, smell and textures, and he seemed to understand. She took her time, caressing him with her tongue while she slid her lips up and down his length. He bumped the back of her mouth and she still couldn't take all of him. She quickly wrapped her fingers around his base and stroked the portion that didn't fit inside her mouth.

She couldn't wait to join with him. He'd fill her, stretch her like never before. She shivered at the thought and bobbed her head faster, desperate to watch him lose control.

He only allowed her play for a few minutes before he pulled her to her feet.

"I wasn't finished," she protested breathlessly.

"Next time," he dismissed. "I want to come together."

It was damn hard to argue with that, so she pulled down the covers and crawled onto the bed. He joined her, moving immediately to kneel between her thighs. He paused for a slow, deep kiss, then found her entrance and pushed inside.

She was soaking wet and seriously turned on, but the fullness still made her gasp. "Damn," she whispered, a bit of her arousal receding.

He didn't try to move. Instead, he stayed deep inside her and continued their kisses.

She concentrated on the sensual slide of his tongue and the soft press of his lips. She was tensing and she wasn't sure why.

That wasn't true. She knew why, she just didn't want to ruin this with insecurities and frustration.

Wrapping both arms around her, he rolled them to their sides. Then he drew her leg up to his waist, keeping himself deep inside her. "Talk to me, love. What's wrong? I thought you wanted to share pleasure."

"I do. I'm sorry. I just..."

He gently tilted her face until their gazes met. "You just?"

"I met you yesterday and already I'm in bed with you. This isn't like me. It's happening way too fast."

His gaze searched hers, then he started to pull out.

She gasped and dug in her heel. "Don't! Please, don't. I want to share pleasure with you. In fact, that's why I'm freaking out. I shouldn't want you this badly."

He caressed her back, keeping her snug against his body. "There is no reason for your fear. I would never hurt you. Close your eyes." He kissed each eyelid, making sure she obeyed. "I'm going to form the transfer link. I'll try to be quick, but it might sting a little."

That was all the warning she got before a sharp sting burst deep inside her brain. The sensation was enough to make her gasp, but it faded quickly. Then feelings and sensations flowed into her mind, expanding reality in a way she'd never experienced before. Warmth and affection surrounded her like a blanket, yet she could sense fierce determination and protectiveness too. She'd heard this described by her friends who had bonded, but no one could really understand until they felt it for themselves.

Her breasts pressed against his chest. He was warm and solid. Now she also felt her softer body from his point of view. To him, she seemed tiny, fragile. She'd never thought of herself that way. Their legs entwined and her inner walls snugly encased his shaft. It was intoxicating and slightly disorienting to sense everything all at once.

Slowly tuning out the physical sensations, she concentrated on the emotions curling and twisting through her mind. His arousal was tightly leashed. Despite his body's urgent demands, he was determined to give her all the time she needed to accept what she was feeling. His selflessness soothed her, melted her inhibitions.

Xorran wasn't interested in a few hours of mutual pleasure. He was desperate to claim her. Winning her heart, her trust, was literally the most important thing in his universe.

Humbled by the realization, she relaxed in his arms. There was no pretending, no way to lie. She literally felt what he felt. "This is amazing."

He rewarded her with more soft kisses while desire and tenderness flowed across their link. "How does this work for you?"

His hips drew back, then he thrust back into her wet core. "Like that."

"No. The link. Do I need to do something to let you in?"

He stilled, his gaze dark and searching. "Do you want me in your mind?"

"Yes," she whispered. "I want this to be interactive."

Clearly pleased with her decision, he smiled from ear to ear. "I was hoping you'd say that."

Suddenly, he swept her beneath him and drew her arms over her head, intertwining their fingers. His gaze never broke contact with hers as he drew back until only his tip remained inside her.

She held her breath, unable to move, barely able to think. There was no need for words. She felt his hunger and the driving urgency of his desire. He controlled his body through sheer force of will, determined to make this good for her. She'd never experienced anything like it, never imagined that she could inspire such feelings in another person.

Finally, he started moving in earnest, filling her with slow, deep strokes. She drew her legs up along his sides, offering herself completely. His need escalated along with his movements, but tenderness threaded through even his most demanding need. Already he cared for her deeply. It didn't make sense from a human perspective. She didn't believe in love at first sight, but it was impossible to ignore what she felt, what *he* felt for her.

Sensations coursed through her body, surging like blood through her veins. She was so lost in the pleasure she barely registered his presence in her mind. His movements were light and careful, meticulously controlled. She didn't resist him, didn't try to withhold any area of her past. She wanted him to know her as well as she was starting to know him.

His hips pumped faster as he released her hands. He angled one arm beneath her neck, supporting himself on his forearm and knees. Then he slipped his free hand between their bodies and found her clit with his thumb. She gasped, arching into his next thrust.

"That's right, angel. Come for me. I want to feel you come."

The whispered command was so damn sexy, it sent a jolt of sensation straight to her core. Her inner muscles tightened rhythmically and suddenly—almost spontaneously—she was coming. Pleasure pulsed through her body, dragging a startled cry from her mouth. He pushed the pleasure higher with his thumb, drawing every last spasm from her before he shifted positions again.

He rocked back onto his knees, and grasped her hips with both hands, lifting her as he drove forward. She found the mattress with her heels and arched into each of his forceful thrusts. They collided, lost together in the gathering storm. The slap of flesh against flesh echoed in the cabin, a sexual rhythm track, accompanied by their gasps and moans.

His energy blazed in her mind, consuming reality. All she saw was him. All she felt was the pleasure they shared. He took her with possessive fervor, and she reveled in the intensity. One thing became clear in that moment. Xorran was in love with her.

The end came suddenly, bursting through her like a sonic *boom*. She arched clear off the bed, crying out sharply as he drove his entire length deep into her core. He shuddered, clutching her hips against his, while his seed released.

They clung to each other as they drifted back down. He managed to take the majority of his weight on his forearms and knees, but he blanketed her from neck to hips. She panted harshly, too weak to move.

"You all right?" He brushed the hair back from her face as he searched her gaze.

"That was...intense."

He sighed and a hint of shame trickled into her mind. "I'm sorry. I tried to be gentle, but I—"

She covered his lips with her fingertips. "Never hold back on me. I want you to be exactly who you are, nothing more, and nothing less."

He kissed her fingers before she lowered her hand. "Are you still hungry, or should we just sleep?"

"I wouldn't mind a sandwich or something, but I need to get back to Wenny."

His brows drew together and he slowly separated their bodies. "The cub is safely contained. There is no reason for you to sleep on the floor again."

"This is her first night in her new habitat," she argued. "There is no way she's spending it alone."

"Gods save us from stubborn females," he grumbled as he scooted to the edge of the bed. "If you're going back down there, so am I. There is no way my potential mate is spending the night alone in the forest."

"Suit yourself." She grinned while his back was turned. She'd counted on this exact reaction.

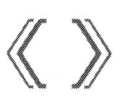

《 》

DR. FORAN DIDN'T COME through with a dart gun until sundown the following night. Xorran and Sara spent the day together, much of the time in Wenny's enclosure. As Xorran feared, word of the cub soon spread and groups of females, and more than a few males, appeared eager for a glimpse of the adorable baby battle cat. For the most part Wenny tolerated the visitors. She basically ignored the females, yet she was hostile to most of the males. Xorran seemed to be the one exception.

"Ask her why she likes me when most other males upset her," he suggested as the sun sank behind the trees.

Sara posed the question in Sarronti and whatever the cub said made her laugh. "According to Wenny, I am strong enough to control you, so she has no reason to fear you."

"I see." He crossed his arms over his chest, trying not to be annoyed by the cub's perspective. "I think Isolaund has given her battle cats a distorted view of life in general."

"Wenny definitely sees Isolaund as the ultimate authority, so it stands to reason that the cats expect the rest of the world to be ruled by females."

"For all we know the Sarronti could be a matriarchal society," he mused. "Alonov clearly has power, but that doesn't mean their Guiding Council isn't populated with females. We simply don't know."

She nodded, but had no comment.

A few minutes later one of Dr. Foran's assistants showed up with the dart gun and six prefilled darts. "We can make more darts if you need them," the tech said, then hurried back toward the Wheel.

Xorran looked over the compact weapon, then tucked it into the back of his pants. "It will be dark in a few minutes. It might be best if we waited until—"

"Not a chance," Sara insisted. "Heather is not spending another night in that place. This has gone on long enough." Her chin came up and her shoulders squared.

He knew that look. Nothing he said would change her mind. "It's almost impossible to find a trail in the dark." It wasn't a lie, just a gross exaggeration. His abilities had nothing to do with the physical world. Energy patterns didn't care if it was day or night.

"Wenny's nose works just as well in the dark. Why do you think so many cat species hunt at night? It gives them an advantage."

"The overlord is right. I'm going to have my hands full with you."

She just laughed and walked over to where the harness and leash were looped around one of the fence posts. Wenny accepted the harness without too much resistance, but fought against the leash as soon as she reached the end of its length. With the cub in tow, they headed for the storeroom where they had slept the night before. They retrieved solar-powered torches and jackets, then headed off through the trees.

"Do you remember where you first saw us in the river?" Sara asked after they hiked for a few minutes.

"Of course. Our introduction was memorable."

She flipped on her torch and lit the ground ahead of them. "Let's follow the river back to that spot, and I'll take it from there."

"Works for me." The ground was uneven and hilly. Even with both torches activated, the forest grew dark fast. He wrapped the handle of Wenny's leash around his wrist and grasped the leash itself. For the most part Wenny tromped along through the underbrush without complaint or resistance. Whenever she ran too far ahead, Sara slowed her with a sharp voice command.

"She is remarkably well-behaved for a wild animal," he concluded.

"She was born in captivity," Sara said. "I'm not sure she still qualifies as wild."

They followed each dip and curve of the river, soon locating the spot where he'd first seen them.

Sara took the lead as they headed deeper into the forest. Trees closed in on them, becoming almost oppressive. If it weren't for their torches, it would have been completely dark.

"I'm pretty sure it was right around here," she insisted a few minutes later. "I remember that rock formation and that cluster of fallen logs."

Wenny sniffed the air, then pulled back her teeth in what looked like a painful grimace. "Is she okay?"

Sara glanced at the cub and said, "She's fine."

"Then what is she doing?"

"On Earth cats have a sensitive olfactory gland in the roof of their mouth. It's called the vomeronasal sac or Jacobson's gland. The expression she just made is called the flehmen reaction. They suck air into their mouths, so the gland can identify territory markings and potential threats."

"Earth's cats smell through their mouths?"

She smiled. "Basically. Apparently karrons do too." She nodded toward the cub who was still making the strange face.

Suddenly, Wenny detected something that excited her. She took off so fast it nearly ripped his hand off. He ran after her, but even Sara's commands were ignored. Wenny headed straight toward a clump of bushes and pawed insistently at the ground.

So much for his holo-shield concept. Those bushes were definitely real.

Wenny growled and whined, looking back at Sara beseechingly.

"She keeps saying 'home' and 'mother'. This has to be it."

They searched the bushes for a trigger or control panel, but found only spindly branches and prickly leaves. "There's nothing here," he muttered, frustrated by their apparent failure.

But Wenny kept vocalizing and digging, clearly convinced she was in the right place.

He slowly circled the bushes, looking at them from every direction. They looked like ordinary shrubs, so what was causing Wenny's reaction?

"Have you lost your mind!"

Xorran snapped his head around and found a beautiful elf female glaring at them. She had pale hair that flowed to her hips and flashing, shimmering eyes. Her coloring was lost in the dimness. Was her hair silver or blue? Was this Isolaund or—

He understood her! Why could he suddenly understand Sarronti?

"Arrista," Sara said with a guilty smile.

Wenny rushed up to the elf and greeted her with a happy figure-eight around her legs. Arrista paused to pet the cub. So this was the servant, not the master.

"Why are you back here?" The question snapped with demand as Arrista straightened. "You promised to keep Weniffa safe. If you had been detected by the guards, Wenny's life would be forfeit."

"I'm worried about Heather." Sara didn't switch to Sarronti. Smart. No need to reveal her new ability when Arrista could understand English.

"Your red friend is safe. We have hidden her where even General Alonov will not go."

"Take me there," Sara said firmly.

"No." The elf glared at Sara, undeterred by her demand. "You will wait until Lady Isolaund contacts you again. She has agreed to the prisoner exchange, but the Guiding Council must approve the action. They never do anything quickly."

"I have only your word that Heather is safe," Sara pointed out. "I want to see her."

"We have only your word that Weniffa is safe, and yet here you are. We are not the ones acting dishonorably."

"How did you know we were out here?" he asked Arrista. Her sudden appearance seemed suspect.

She looked at him, arching brows raised. Then she asked Sara what he'd said. She really couldn't understand English without the translator link.

"Can you understand my words?" the elf asked.

If they ever wanted Arrista to trust them, they needed to be truthful with her. He nodded. "I don't know how, but yes. I know what you're saying."

Sara translated and Arrista's eyes narrowed. She looked from him to Sara and back. "Are you two intimate?"

He nodded, refusing to offer details.

"Translation *lenitas* are aggressive, but harmless. They often pass from body to body with intimate activities." He felt a faint ping inside his mind, and then she said, "I will be able to understand you now."

"Thanks for the explanation." But she hadn't answered his question. "How did you know we were here?"

"All of Isolaund's cats are tagged. Their *lenitas* are locator beacons, but they also serve other purposes. Wenny set off a perimeter alarm. Luckily for you, Isolaund is in with the Guiding Council, so I saw the warning light instead of her. I reset the alarm, but it will keep going off until Wenny is out of range. You need to leave now!"

"Come with us," Sara offered suddenly. "Your life would be very different if you leave the Underground."

Arrista sucked in a breath and pressed her hand to her throat. "I cannot...it's impossible."

Sara moved closer, advancing with slow yet steady strides. "It's not. Our home would protect you from the sunlight and you would no longer be anyone's slave."

The elf lowered her arm as her head tilted up. "I am not a slave. I serve Lady Isolaund by choice."

"You told me those in your designation have no control over anything," Sara reminded. "That sounds like slavery to me. Our men fought a war in order to escape such attitudes."

"Just go."

Arrista's shimmering gaze shifted to him and he saw the conflict in her eyes. He'd thought Sara was being melodramatic, but her instincts were right on the mark. Arrista was seriously tempted by the offer, yet something powerful held her back.

"If you're not ready to escape, then help us," Sara urged. "We do not want a war with your people. Educate us. Tell us how to avoid the coming fight."

The elf shook her head and lowered her gaze. "It cannot be stopped. It has already begun." Without another word, she stepped out of the stream of light coming from his torch and melted into the darkness. "Damn it."

"We're obviously close." Sara sounded as frustrated as he felt.

"Come on. Let's get Wenny a safe distance away." He started walking, but hit the end of the leash and the cub refused to move.

Sara gave the command for follow. Wenny ignored her, staring longingly at the bushes.

"Wenny we have to go. Now!" Sara repeated the command, but again the cub ignored her.

Xorran tugged on the leash, dragging Wenny across the ground a foot or two. "She's not budging."

"Can you blame her?" She approached the cat slowly, cautiously. "I shouldn't have brought her here. I was thinking of Heather, not Wenny."

Wenny waited until Sara nearly reached her, then turned and bared her teeth, growling with obvious menace.

Sara held up both hands. "I'm not going to hurt you, sweetheart, but we have to get out of here." Slowly, she extended her hand and Wenny snapped at her, sharp teeth coming precariously close to Sara's hand.

"This is pointless." Xorran pulled the dart gun from his pants and shot the cub before Sara had time to object.

Wenny growled and twisted, desperately trying to dislodge the dart.

They had stressed fast-acting when they'd told Dr. Foran what they needed. Apparently, the doctor took them seriously. Within seconds, Wenny's head drooped and she wobbled unsteadily. It took her a bit longer to go under completely, but Xorran was still pleased with the result. He walked over and scooped up the cub.

"Sorry, love," he said to Sara. "We don't have time for a battle of wills."

Mercifully, Sara didn't argue. She followed him through the trees, rushing to keep up with his long strides. They reached the river without incident, and Sara took the lead.

"Is she still breathing? She went out awfully fast."

He paused to watch the rise and fall of Wenny's fury chest. "She's fine. Stop worrying."

"It's my job to worry about her," Sara grumbled.

When they reached the enclosure, the overlord was waiting for them. And he was clearly angry.

"What were you hoping to accomplish by this little stunt?" the overlord demanded, standing in front of the gate.

Xorran shifted the cub higher against his chest and widened his stance. He needn't have bothered.

Sara moved in front of the overlord and motioned Xorran toward the enclosure. Though she hadn't spoken, her message was clear, *Get Wenny settled while I take care of this.*

"Wenny helped us identify the location of an entrance," she told Kage in a calm, clear voice. "Unfortunately, we weren't able to activate the door."

"And what if you had?" the overlord challenged. "A tracker and an unarmed female were going to take on the elves?"

Sara put her hands on her hips, clearly ready for an argument. "We weren't going to take on anyone. It was a recon mission. We were going to locate Heather and then determine our next action based on her exact situation."

Xorran nearly laughed as he carefully placed Wenny in her shelter. They hadn't really had a plan beyond finding Heather, but the overlord didn't need to know.

"If you weren't able to open the door, how do you know you found the entrance? Could you actually see the door?" Kage persisted.

"Wenny grew very excited and clawed at the ground. And she kept saying 'home' and 'mother.'"

The overlord snorted as he folded his arms over his chest. "I wasn't aware that karrons could speak."

"She's telepathic," she said emphatically.

"Gods above, you're serious." He moved closer to the enclosure, looking at Wenny with new interest. "Is that how Isolaund controls them? She can actually reason with them?"

"I'm not sure reason is involved. More like loyalty through fear. The battle cats are pampered and fed well. And staying in her favor ensures their progeny an opportunity to be trained as well. But if they fail her, they're discarded like rubbish. She has abandoned entire bloodlines because of the failure of one cat."

"The servant told you all of this?"

She shook her head. "Wenny did."

"What else have you learned from your new pet?" His gaze narrowed and his expression sharpened. "How many elves are there really? How large is their army? Do they have access to spacecraft?"

Again, she shook her head. "Wenny won't tell me anything that endangers the elves. As I said, she is extremely loyal, despite the fact that Isolaund sent her away."

His only response was a thoughtful grunt.

"We saw Arrista again," Sara told him. "Wenny's locator chip set off some sort of alarm."

"Wenny has a locator chip?" His scowl returned in a flash.

"The elves already know where to find us," she pointed out. "It's not like we're hiding from them."

"Did anyone else know you were snooping around?"

"No," she assured him. "Arrista turned off the alarm before anyone else saw it. I tried to convince her to defect, but she isn't ready."

Xorran joined them near the gate, though he stood on the inside of the fence. "She might never be ready, Sara. Like the cub, Arrista is strangely loyal to Isolaund."

"That's not unusual. Slaves are often so beaten down they can't comprehend a life free of bondage. Besides, she would be much more valuable to us as a spy than a refugee." The overlord looked at Xorran as he asked, "Can you find the entrance without the cat?"

"Easily. But the door is undetectable."

Kage shrugged. "It might not be for Torrin."

Why did the overlord always think of Torrin when he needed assistance? "What can he do that we didn't try already?"

He started to speak, then changed his mind. "That's Torrin's story to tell."

"May I ask a question, sir." Xorran knew the overlord responded best to respect freely given.

"Of course."

"How did you know where we'd gone? We weren't gone that long."

"Dr. Foran mentioned the dart gun in his latest report. I dropped by to ask you about it and all three of you were MIA. It didn't take much to figure out where you'd gone." He looked at Sara and shook his head. "Your mate isn't known for her patience."

"Arrista assured us that Heather is safe from Alonov, so I'm hoping that will settle Sara down."

Sara scoffed. "Not likely."

The overlord laughed. "I'm so glad she's yours, not mine. Get her back to the Wheel as soon as possible. It's not safe for you two to be out here alone."

"Wenny will protect us," Sara's tone was just sarcastic enough that Xorran wasn't sure if she was serious or not.

"Not from Isolaund she won't," the overlord's tone hardened, all friendliness gone "I'm serious. I want you both inside the Wheel within the hour."

"Yes, sir," she muttered, sounding more frustrated than facetious.

The overlord left without further discussion.

"You really shouldn't piss him off. He can be one mean son of a bitch."

"Not to a female," she predicted. "I can see it in his eyes."

"Well, he could easily make my life miserable, so I'm asking you nicely to behave."

She smiled. "Since you asked so nicely, I'll try."

Chapter Seven

Word from the elves didn't arrive for another three days. Sara was so angry with the delay that she wanted to scream. If it hadn't been for Arrista's insistence that Heather was safely stashed where Alonov couldn't find her, Sara would have tried again to sneak into the Underground. With or without Xorran's assistance.

Just the thought of Xorran helped calm her. He was the perfect combination of fierce protectiveness and patience. They'd spent the last three days together only separating for short periods of time. Sara had lunch with Thea and Lily on the second day, and Xorran had to update the high command yesterday. Other than that, they had been side by side, or in other interesting positions. Each time they shared pleasure—she decided she liked the Rodyte phrase better than human euphemisms—was more wonderful than the last. The transfer link created a closeness that was simply not possible with two humans. She felt like she'd known him for years, not days.

"The elf contingent will be here at dusk," Xorran told her.

"They better bring Heather with them or this could be another stall tactic."

"We're aware," Xorran sighed. "The overlord wants you there. He thinks it will be good for Heather and he wants you to verify what they say."

She nodded. "I'll do it for Heather, but you'll have to restrain me if they start playing games."

They gathered by the barracks at sundown, not wanting the elves too close to the Wheel.

The overlord was decked out in his barbarian costume, snug black pants, long red cape, heavily tattooed chest bare. Thick munitions belts crossed his torso, and the sides of the cape were thrown back, giving him easy access to his weapons. Sara had only seen him like this once before and she had to admit it made him look incredibly mean.

A purple haze fell over the scene as the sun sank below the horizon. The overlord paced beside Wenny's enclosure and the cub followed him, batting playfully at his billowing cape. Suddenly, Wenny stopped and her head cocked, then she let out a mournful cry. Seconds later a louder, deeper call echoed in the distance. Wenny clawed at the fence, then balanced on her back legs as she banged with her front paws.

Sara hurried over to her. "What's wrong, baby?"

Momma come. Momma come. The thought shoved into Sara's mind with graceless enthusiasm.

Sara turned around just in time to watch Isolaund emerge from the forest. Her dark green hooded cloak concealed her hair and most of her body, but Sara recognized her sharp features and ice-cold stare. Not to mention the massive battle cat walking at her side. Was that Wenny's mother? The karron was huge, and heavily armored, striding along with lethal grace.

This was a prisoner exchange. Why did Isolaund need a *battle* cat?

Well, to be fair, the overlord was armed to the teeth and had his best warriors stashed in the trees surrounding them. Clearly trust was an issue on both sides.

Momma! Go see Momma!

Isolaund's battle cat turned her head sharply and called a throaty greeting to her cub. Wenny ran the length of her enclosure and back, too excited to remain still.

Reaching down, Isolaund stroked the battle cat's head, then spoke a word Sara didn't understand. Immediately the battle cat turned her head back around and stared straight ahead. Clearly she'd been reprimanded for her behavior.

Not wanting to draw undue attention to Wenny, Sara said, "*Deztee.*" Then she raised her right hand and made a fist.

Wenny stilled and her excited vocalizations stopped, but telepathically she persisted, *Go home? Momma take home? Please!*

The cub's blue eyes pleaded right along with her sweet mind voice and Sara fought back tears. *This is your home, baby. You need to stay with me.*

Wenny's only response was a forlorn little cry.

Sara was so distracted by the upset karron that she barely noticed General Alonov. He wore sculpted armor and a variety of weapons, not unlike the overlord. His golden gaze narrowed as he looked around. "Where is my son?" he asked in Sarronti.

Isolaund repeated the question in English.

"He will be released as soon as I see Heather. Where is she?" the overlord responded in a calm, even tone. Despite his outward stillness, his dark gaze took in everything.

"We felt it essential to set some ground rules before we make the actual exchange," Isolaund told him.

"Until I see Heather, know that she is alive and unharmed, we have nothing to talk about."

"Fine." She huffed, flipping back her cape. Her simple gown was heavily embroidered with metallic thread. The colors were undetectable in the dimness, but moonlight made the pattern gleam. She slid her fingers along her forearm, then made a curving gesture with her hand.

A life-sized image of Heather appeared between Isolaund and the overlord. Heather looked around, confusion clearly written on her face. "Hello," she called. "Is someone there?"

"She can hear us, but cannot see us," Isolaund explained. "Speak to her if you must. The signal can be undependable at this range."

Which meant Heather was not nearby.

"Heather, this is Kage Razel. Are you okay? Have you been abused in anyway?"

"Oh please, get me out of here! Where are you?"

"You'll be released soon, but I need to know that you're unharmed."

"Scared, filthy, and royally pissed off, but they haven't really hurt me." An instant after the words left her mouth, her image blinked off.

"You have your confirmation." Isolaund shrugged and her cloak swished forward, concealing her body again. "Now may we speak candidly?"

Alonov muttered something Sara couldn't hear.

Isolaund nodded, then looked at Kage. "We require the same assurance. We need to see Farlo."

"Torak," the overlord called out and the burly warlord walked out of the barracks, his fist tightly grasping the young elf's upper arm, a pulse pistol pressed to his side.

"Are you well, son? Have they harmed you?" The concern in the general's tone contradicted his war-hardened appearance.

"I'm fine, sir. It takes more than this lot to harm a Sarronti soldier."

Alonov smiled and Torak dragged Farlo back into the barracks.

"We've both agreed to the exchange," Kage said. "I'm not sure what else there is to say."

"You are trespassing on land that belongs to the Sarronti," she said firmly. "We expect you to leave."

"It's my understanding that you are unable to inhabit this land," the overlord's tone was just as insistent. "I consider that a vacancy."

"We are the guardians of this place and you are defiling it!" Her tone rose nearly an octave as her ire escalated. "You have no right to chop down these trees or kill the animals in our forests. Only savages eat flesh." She shuddered violently.

"We've been called worse." When she just glared at him, the overlord said, "If you want to talk boundaries or limitations, I'm willing to negotiate. But leaving is not an option."

Alonov asked what Kage was saying, so Isolaund paused to catch him up.

"Then why do you look so annoyed?" the general asked once she had finished. "The council wants us to negotiate. That's why we're here."

She made an exasperated sound and turned back to Kage. "The far side of the planet is somewhat dry, but we might be able to tolerate your presence over there."

The overlord laughed, a harsh, hallow sound. "The far side of this planet is a wasteland. We'll stay right where we are."

"Then so will Heather," she sneered.

"You already agreed to the exchange." His tone was so tight it sounded like he was gritting his teeth.

"I changed my mind," she snapped and whirled around, cloak fanning out around her. With a heartrending glance at her cub, the battle cat followed her mistress into the trees.

Alonov rushed after Isolaund, demanding to know what had been said.

"That bitch," Kage snarled. "She had no intention of making the exchange."

"Then why bother coming at all?" Xorran asked.

"I'm not sure. Maybe she was sizing us up, maybe getting a better look at our encampment." He called out to Torak and told him to take Farlo back to the *Viper*.

"This is all Isolaund," Sara told them. "Alonov asked why she was arguing, said the council sent them here to negotiate with us."

Kage nodded, looking thoughtful rather than angry. "This is personal with her. We need to access the council directly. Isolaund will sabotage us at every turn."

"Then how do we get Heather back?" Sara cried. "Isolaund controls her."

Kage looked at Xorran. "I've had enough of this shit. I want you, Torrin and Torak to go get her. Torrin should be able to get you in, Torak can fight off any guards, and you will be able to locate her." He sighed. "I guess that should have been a question. If Torrin and Torak assist you, will you be able to find Heather?"

"I'll sure as hells give it my best shot."

"Good. Then figure out what you need to make this happen. I'll send the others to you as soon as they're free."

"Understood."

The overlord strode off toward the Wheel and Sara realized she hadn't had a part in the escape plan. "I'm just supposed to stay here and pet Wenny?"

"Yes," Xorran said firmly. "Isolaund is spoiling for a fight. This could get ugly fast. I don't want you anywhere near any of it."

"But I went last time," she pointed out.

"That was recon. We were assessing the situation, nothing more."

Wenny made a forlorn sound that tore at Sara's heart. The cub had been pacing the fence line or digging at the ground ever since Isolaund stormed off with her battle cat at her side.

Momma, come back. Momma, pleeease!

"Go on." He carefully opened the gate and Sara slipped inside the enclosure. "Your baby needs you."

He was right. Clearly Wenny was devastated to be separated yet again, but Sara also knew he was using it as a distraction.

《 》

TORRIN AND TORAK ARRIVED about an hour later. They discussed strategy for a few minutes, then headed out. The plan was simple. Get in, find Heather, get out as quickly and quietly as possible. Their hope was to remain undetected, but each was heavily armed just in case. Xorran led them through the forest with new confidence. He knew he could find the location, but he still had no idea how Torrin was going to activate the opening when no one else could.

It was fully dark by the time they reached the small clearing. They carried handheld torches, but kept them pointed toward the ground. Xorran motioned to the cluster of bushes. "This is the area where Wenny reacted. We searched everywhere but couldn't find the door." Challenge crept into his tone, but the assassin just smiled.

Without a word of explanation, Torrin splayed his fingers and ran them over and around each bush. Did he have some sort of subdermal scanner? What in creation's name was he doing?

"Aha, very clever." He pressed on a section of dirt directly under one of the bushes and Xorran heard a strange hissing pop. Inset slightly beneath the bush, the trigger was obviously meant to be activated with the foot. Suddenly the rock formation directly behind the bushes undulated, then dissolved.

"I'll be damned," Xorran muttered. "How did you find that?"

Torrin stood and brushed off his knees. "Trade secret. If I told you, I'd have to kill you, and I rather like you."

Torak rolled his eyes. "He's a freaking cyborg." The warlord shoved Torrin aside, drew his weapon, and headed into the opening.

"I was born, not manufactured," Torrin stressed in an angry whisper. "I am *not* a cyborg."

Maybe not, but he was no ordinary hybrid either. "Are all of your powers technology-based or were you born with abilities?"

"Later," the warlord urged, motioning them to advance.

Xorran nodded and followed the bigger male into the stone passageway. It was dark and dank, rounded like a tunnel. All three males had to hunch over because of the limited space. Torrin was directly behind them. Xorran could sense the assassin, but he moved silently. The more Xorran learned about the assassin, the more fascinating he became.

The passageway angled downward and the temperature dropped steadily as they descended. The coolness felt nice after the heat and humidity on the surface, but this wasn't a leisure exploration. They had a job to do.

Xorran drew energy into his center and activated his empathic receptors. Tuning out everything but his objective, he scanned outward in slowly expanding pulses of energy. Heather had been afraid and angry. He searched for that combination and the basic energy pattern shared by humankind. Each race felt different and each individual was a variation on that theme. There was only one human in the Underground, so she wasn't hard to find. Unfortunately, she wasn't alone either.

"This way," he urged as they reached the next corner.

Torak looked at him uncertainly but followed.

Xorran hurried his pace. Fear was rapidly eroding her other emotions. He ran, no longer trying to be silent. He turned down one corridor and then another. As he came to an intersection, he heard voices, so he stopped his companions with an upraised hand, and waited until the small group of elves passed in the adjacent corridor.

Heather was below them he realized as her signal grew stronger. Frantically searching, he found a wooden ladder and climbed down, then headed back in the direction they'd just come.

"Are you sure you know where you're going?" Torak's voice was harsh and impatient. "We're backtracking."

Focused entirely on Heather, Xorran didn't bother answering. Heather's fear assailed him in sickening waves. He rounded the final corner and a shrill scream confirmed his destination.

He lunged into a dank chamber very different from the rest of the cave. His boots slid on the slimy stone floor and undulating light reflected off the pool on the far side of the room. Fury detonated inside him, propelled by vivid memories. He took in the all too familiar scene with one assessing glance. Heather huddled against the wall, legs drawn up to her chest, tears streaming down her grimy face. Alonov stood nearby, grabbling with Arrista.

"The council forbade this!" Arrista yelled, stubbornly hanging off one of Alonov's arms.

"Keep it up and you're next!" the general shot back, but she still wouldn't let go. He swung his other arm, punching her squarely in the face.

Fucking bastard! Xorran threw himself across the room, vision hazed red. Arrista moaned, hands slipping as she sank to the floor. Xorran shoved Alonov away from the women, then punched him as hard as he could. The general grunted, head snapping to one side. But he shook off the blow and attacked with a flurry of punishing jabs. Xorran absorbed the pain with practiced ease. Physical abuse was nothing new. This bastard needed to die! He pulled back his arm, ready to continue the fight, when a pulse of energy streamed past his cheek. The shot hit Alonov in the chest. He shrieked, shuddered, then collapsed in a graceless heap.

Xorran left him where he fell and turned around. The warlord returned his pulse pistol to the bracket on his thigh and swung Heather up into his arms. Torrin was already holding Arrista, who hung limply in his embrace. Heather clung to Torak's neck, weeping like a terrified child. She was rather young. Her hysteria was to be expected. Arrista was clearly unconscious, apparently knocked out by the general's punch.

"Head out," Xorran urged. "I'll cover you." He glanced once at the fallen general. Would killing him make matters worse?

"Are you coming?" The warlord called.

Xorran nodded and they jogged back the way they'd come. Xorran ran behind the others, his weapon now in his hand. Heather eagerly climbed up the ladder, but Arrista made the trip draped over Torrin's shoulder. They were nearly to the entrance when a pair of guards spotted them.

"Run!" Xorran fired first, drawing the elves' attention while the others sprinted for the exit. Xorran ducked behind a jutting rock formation and fired at each guard in turn. One fell with the first volley, but the other was far more skilled. He mirrored Xorran's movements and matched him shot for shot.

Opening his empathic receptors wide, Xorran locked onto the elf, waiting for the surge of emotion that would indicate his next offensive. This was a tactic Xorran had perfected over seemingly endless battles. He was thankful for the skill right now. The elf dove to the side, abandoning his cover just long enough to shoot. But Xorran was ready for him. He fired half a second before the elf, then barely rolled out of the way of the elf's energy stream. The elf fell to the stone floor with a muffled cry and Xorran didn't look back. He ran as fast as his legs could move and burst from the opening into the forest.

The rest of his team was nowhere in sight. Good. The females were their top priority.

Flipping on his torch, he ran through the forest, the path somewhat familiar now. He found the river and was able to run faster along the grassy bank. The Wheel had just come into sight by the time he caught up to the others.

"Are they on your tail?" Torak asked, his voice gruff and commanding.

"No. There were only two and I incapacitated both."

"Good job," Torak muttered, high praise for the stoic warlord.

Arrista was awake now, but seemed content in Torrin's arms.

"We're headed to main medical," Torak told Xorran. "Go update Kage."

"Will do." He asked the computer the location of the overlord and was directed to the war room, aka Kage's office, on deck five. The door slid open as he approached and Xorran's steps faltered when he found Sara sitting across the planning table from the overlord. "Is everything all right?"

She smiled at him and patted the seat next to hers.

"Your stubborn mate refused to leave the cub, so I took her into protective custody." Kage told him with an unapologetic smile. "You really do need to get control of your female."

"I'm trying, sir. I assure you."

"The best ones are always hard to break," the overlord said.

"The best ones refuse to be broken," Sara countered.

"I'll take your word for it. The last thing I need is a female to complicate my life."

"You don't intend to claim a mate?" she sounded horribly offended. "How can you expect something of your men that you refuse to do yourself? That's hypocritical."

"She has a point." Xorran slipped onto the raised chair and grabbed the back of hers, a possessive motion he couldn't stop.

Kage shrugged. "I know, but now is not the time. Is Heather free?"

"He's back," Sara pointed out. "Of course she's free." Then she looked at Xorran. "Where is she?"

Pleased by her vote of confidence, he replied, "Main medical. She's unharmed, thanks to Arrista. Who is also in main medical, by the way."

"Did the elf come of her own free will or was she...persuaded?" Kage wanted to know.

"Alonov was trying to force himself on Heather when we arrived. Arrista fought him off, or at least she was trying very hard to. He punched her in the face for her effort. She was unconscious when we left, so I don't know if this will please her or not."

Kage thought for a moment, then shook his head. "Alonov would have killed her for interfering. You had no choice but to bring her along."

"I agree, but I'm not sure she will." He looked at Sara. "Arrista won't understand anyone unless she links with them, and it's doubtful she'd feel safe enough to do so."

She slipped off her chair with a nod. "We better get down there. She must be terrified."

"Keep Sara in the Wheel," Kage called as the headed out the door. "I do not what her sleeping out by the enclosure!"

The door slid closed before Xorran could reply, so he took Sara's hand and they went to the clinic.

"Did you guys make it in and out without being seen?" she wanted to know.

"Almost. A couple of guards spotted us, but we were nearly out by then."

"What did you do?" She looked up at him, concern creasing her brow. "You're not hurt, are you?" She pulled him to a stop and looked him over for telltale bandages.

"I'm fine, love. All five of us are fine. Well, Arrista has a split lip and a nasty bruise, but that's easily repaired."

"I can't believe that bastard punched her hard enough to knock her out. What a jerk."

"I think the reason he was there is proof enough of his utter lack of character." He took her by the hand and they continued on their way.

"Agreed."

They reached the clinic and found it buzzing with conversations and activity. Victims from a minor explosion were being treated on one side of the round room while Arrista, Heather, and a horde of concerned males had congregated on the other. Heather was basking in the attention, so Sara made a beeline for the elf.

Arrista sat on one of the treatment tables, legs drawn up to her chest. Her eyes were round as saucers and her entire body trembled. Torrin stood beside her, clearly trying to calm her fear, but nothing he said had any effect on the traumatized female.

The elf spotted Sara and came alive. "Oh, Sara, thank the gods. Please tell them I was trying to protect Heather. I am no threat to anyone."

Sara rushed to the opposite side of the bed from Torrin and gently took Arrista's hand. "You're not our prisoner. The men were worried that General Alonov would harm you, so they brought you here. You can return if that's what you want, but we really wish you would consider staying, at least for a while."

Shifting her gaze from Sara, to Torrin, to Xorran and back, Arrista seemed to consider her options. "Does that male belong to you?" She made a subtle motion toward Xorran.

"Yes." Sara looked at him and smiled. "That's my mate."

His heart flipped over in his chest. Was she accepting his claim, or just simplifying the situation for Arrista?

"And this one?" Arrista asked.

"I belong to no one," Torrin said firmly in Sarronti.

Arrista gasped. "Why can you suddenly speak my language? You did not do so before?"

"He's accessing my translator," Sara told her. "I have to be nearby for him to do it."

"I can resolve that issue, if your friend is willing," Dr. Foran said. He stood slightly back, apparently waiting for a break in the conversation. Everyone looked at him expectantly, so he explained, "We got lucky with your blood sample," he told Sara. "We were able to isolate one of their nanites, and our biotech team has been analyzing it ever since. I can inject her with one of our translators. I believe the two will operate separately, without interfering with each other."

"Is Rodyte tech safe for the Sarronti?" Challenge rippled through Sara's tone.

"Obviously, this has never been tried with a Sarronti, but I have injected sixty-eight different species with these nanites and none had an adverse reaction."

Sara turned back to Arrista and explained what Dr. Foran had said.

"How does this translator know my language?" the elf wanted to know.

Good question. They all looked at Foran as Sara asked the question in Rodyte.

He smiled, apparently pleased with himself. "I recorded Farlo Alonov and channeled the audio stream into our linguistic computer. He likes to talk to himself when he thinks no one is listening."

Sara translated for Arrista and the elf smiled. "Tell the doctor that I will allow the injection."

Dr. Foran administered the nanites, then went back to his other patients. Arrista was chatting away in Rodyte in no time at all. She was still cautious, and strangely focused on Torrin, which was making the assassin uncomfortable.

"I need to get back to work," he said suddenly. "Welcome to OP3." The greeting had been meant for Arrista, but he didn't make eye contact with her before hurrying from the room.

"OP3?" Sara asked.

"Outcast Planet 3," Xorran told her. "The high command has been calling it that for weeks and it seems to have caught on."

"This planet is Sarronti, not OP3," Arrista insisted.

He and Sara just nodded, then Sara said, "I get the OP part, but what's with the 3?"

"This was the third planet we seriously considered." He chuckled. "Maybe we should have stuck with 2."

Arrista seemed somewhat settled, so they moved over to check on Heather. Her face had been scrubbed clean, though her hair was still in need of shampoo. She smiled at Sara, then introduced her to the three males lined up on the other side of the treatment table. "These are my suitors." A bright blush broke out on the crest of her cheeks, making her look even younger.

"I see," Sara said, returning the younger woman's smile. According to Sara, Heather had been crushed when her potential mates didn't immediately begin courting her. Apparently, her peril was the kick in the ass they needed to come out of the shadows. "I just wanted to make sure you were okay. Looks like you're in good hands."

Heather's only reply was another shy smile.

"Let's go," Sara tugged on his sleeve, urging him toward the exit.

More than happy to be alone with his soon-to-be mate, Xorran wrapped his arm around her and headed for his cabin.

Chapter Eight

"Kage told me he'd set up a surveillance feed, so I can keep an eye on Wenny without endangering myself," Sara told Xorran as they reached his cabin.

"It's a great idea, but when did the overlord become Kage to you?" Xorran did not sound happy with the development.

Jealousy, in small measures, was flattering, and Sara allowed herself a pleased smile. "Kage also assured me that the communication ban will be lifted, so I'll be able to do video conferences with my family."

"I'm thrilled to hear it. Stop calling him Kage."

She laughed. "He's a nice guy and you know it, so stop scowling at me."

"He's a ruthless killer, and you know it. Don't let his charm fool you. It's one of many weapons in his arsenal."

She sighed. "I've heard the stories, but they're hard to believe once you've spent time with him."

"They aren't stories, love. At least not most of them. I've never seen him in action, but Torak certainly has and he willingly bows to the overlord's authority. The only reason he'd do that is because the overlord is even more deadly than he is."

"Fine. We'll agree to disagree on the subject of Kage Razel." She waved away the topic as she went to the sofa and sat down.

"Tell me about the raid. How in blazes did Torrin open the door?"

Xorran joined her on the couch before he began his explanation. "There is much more to Torrin than meets the eye. Torak called him a cyborg, though Torrin objected to the label."

"A cyborg? If he has a bunch of robotic parts, they're certainly concealed well."

He stretched out his arm along the sofa's padded back, his fingertips lightly stroking the nape of her neck. "He...scanned the area with his hand and located a foot trigger. He wasn't using any sort of equipment, so I can only conclude that he *is* the scanner."

"How strange. He looks completely—" She laughed and shook her head. "I almost said human. It's so easy to forget that none of you are." He moved his entire hand to her neck and gently squeezed, massaging the tense muscles. She moaned. "Do that for five minutes and I'll be asleep."

Immediately he stopped and tangled his fingers in her hair. "Can't have that. I'm not finished with you yet."

She poked him in the side. "You are unless you take a shower. You reek of sweat."

"Fair enough." He stood and stripped off his shirt. "Get naked and get in bed."

Her brows arched at his bossy tone. "And if I don't?"

"Stay right there and you'll find out," he warned, then walked into the bathroom, which could be accessed from the living room or the bedroom.

The rebellious part of Sara wanted to test him, but common sense won out. The last thing she wanted was conflict.

Their relationship should be a haven, a shelter from the rest of the world—or worlds.

She went into the bedroom and undressed, then slipped into bed, propping herself up against the sleek headboard. Sonic showers were much faster than water, so she was sure he would choose that option. A few minutes later, he opened the door and walked into the bedroom buck naked.

"Wise decision," he praised. His features were tight, gaze intense.

"Are you always like this after a mission?" She licked her lips, heart thudding wildly. "I'm not sure if I like it or not."

He chuckled, but his fierce expression didn't soften. "This is why so many babies are born nine months after a battle." He ripped the sheet from under her hand and crawled onto the bed.

She gasped, then giggled, horrified that such a childish sound had just released from her throat. If she didn't know him as well as she did, this aggression would have been frightening. Instead her nipples peaked and her clit tingled in response to his obvious need.

He grabbed her ankles and pulled her down the bed, until she lay flat on her back. Then he moved over her, wedging his knees between her thighs. "I need you." The words sounded gravelly, his tone even deeper than usual.

Rather than speak, she opened her legs and bent her knees.

He growled in response to her offer and found her entrance with the tip of his cock. Her body had just started to respond, so she hissed when he tried to push inside. She was wet, but apparently not wet enough to take his girth.

Crawling off the end of the bed, he knelt on the deck and pulled her hips to the edge of the mattress. With one quick motion he draped her legs over his broad shoulders and buried his face between her legs. He wasn't gentle or finessed as he usually was when he aroused her with his mouth. He thrust his tongue into her core over and over, claiming her with possessive jabs.

She tilted her hips and stroked his hair, thrilled by his abandon. This was the savage side of Xorran that she sensed but never saw, and she wanted to know all of him. Their link came alive and emotions, raw and consuming flowed into her mind. Desire, bonfire hot, burned through her consciousness, making her gasp and moan. The pull could be intense, but this was different, darker, rooted somewhere in his past.

Mine. The word echoed through his soul, part demand, part plea. She opened her mind to him, offering her being as freely as she offered her body. He surged across the link, drinking in her emotions, soothing himself with her affection. And her surrender.

Gradually, he calmed. The frantic urgency eased and he remembered why he was down there. He pulled back slightly, brushing her folds with his lips. She let out her breath slowly, not trusting his new mood. His tongue gently traced her slit, teasing, caressing.

She held perfectly still and focused on the sensations building beneath his lips. Whatever demon that had been driving him was contained for the time being. His hands slid up and down her legs while his tongue explored her folds. His refusal to touch her clit drew restlessness to the surface. The rest felt nice, but she needed his tongue right there, circling and flicking the sensitive knot of nerves.

"Please, Xorran."

Please, what? Instead of lifting his mouth from her sex, he pushed the question into her mind.

Why did males insist on making females beg for pleasure? It was so annoying. She knew the answer. Exerting control over their mate's body made them feel powerful. Well, she needed an orgasm badly, so starting a fight would be foolish. "Lick my clit," she whispered. "Make me come."

If he'd tried to make her say please, he'd probably get kicked in the face. Luckily for both, he left it alone and gave her what she needed. His lips closed around her clit and sucked ever so gently. She moaned deep in her throat as pleasure swelled and twisted through her core. Then his tongue circled the ultrasensitive nub, teasing it with all the skill and patience she'd come to expect from him.

The orgasm built slowly, like a storm hovering on the horizon. She raised her arms over her head and just let go. He pushed two fingers into her sopping-wet center, thrusting in and out, while he continued to tease her clit. She tightened her inner muscles, pushing the tension higher. His lips suddenly closed around her again and she came with a startled cry. Sharp yet blissful sensations pulsed through her abdomen, blurring her surroundings until her mind was incapable of thought.

He shifted her legs to the bend of his elbows as he surged to his feet. This time when he tried to enter, she accepted him easily. They both moaned as his length filled her completely. Unable to restrain himself a millisecond longer, he pulled his hips back, then thrust back in, burying himself to the balls in one sharp move.

"Yes," she gasped. "Hard. Make it hard."

Xorran chuckled as he continued his slow, deep thrusts. "I don't think it's ever been harder," he teased. He wanted to pound into her like a madman, but it had to be his idea. He felt raw and restless, savage in a way he hadn't felt in years. The mission, though a success, brought up unwanted memories.

Refusing to be distracted by the past, he focused on Sara's lovely face. She had her arms raised overhead and her gaze was unfocused. She was so damn beautiful she didn't seem quite real. Then her inner muscles tightened around his surging cock and reality returned with a vengeance. His balls burned and his shaft ached, his need to come literally painful.

He kept her legs hooked over his arms as he reached up and grasped her waist. Then he sped his thrusts, giving her fast and hard, because now it was his idea. She arched and wiggled, completely lost in the sensual storm. Her mind was open and accepting, a rare gift he would cherish always.

Deeper and harder, he took her, until his control finally snapped. He ended with a super-fast flurry of thrusts that made release impossible to withhold. He dropped his head back and closed his eyes as pleasure blasted through his body. He gasped, holding her still while he jetted deep inside her.

She came half a second later, the rippling pulsation of her core, drawing him deeper into her body. He shuddered and she shivered, wrapping her legs around his waist. "'He's got to be fresh from the fight,'" she whispered with a dreamy smile. "Okay. I get it now."

"What?" Her words made no sense.

She laughed, her body tightening around his with each chuckle. "It's a song. My mother used to sing it whenever she wanted to annoy my dad. It's about finding a man who's brave and fierce, and not afraid to fight for the woman he loves. All the things my father was not."

"Why did she marry him if he lacked the qualities she desired in a mate?"

"Damn good question." She sighed. "I don't know the answer."

He carefully separated their bodies and joined her on the bed. She generally curled up and went to sleep after they shared pleasure. He wanted to understand why this time had made her talkative and melancholy. "I know they're no longer together. Do you still have a relationship with both, or did you feel obligated to join one side or the other."

"They both behaved so badly during the divorce that I didn't speak to either for almost a year. Then Mom showed up at work. She looked so miserable that I couldn't be mean to her. Dad called a few days later, said if I was going to talk to her it was only fair for me to talk to him. Now I stay in touch with both, but comments about the other one are off limits."

He settled on his back and she curled up against his side, her head pillowed on his shoulder. "I think it's hard for you to be mean to anyone, except the warlord." He grinned, pleased by the memory.

"Torak deserved it. He's a jerk." She pushed up, bracing her upper body on her forearm so she could look at him. "Will one of the human females have to bond with him?"

"I presume. Arton's goal was to give each Outcast at least one match. I guess it's possible that he didn't achieve his goal."

She nodded, then paused, hesitating to broach the next topic. "What was going on with you earlier? The mission obviously upset you. Why?"

He was tempted just to show her, but the memories were so horrendous, he didn't want to subject her to the nightmare. "I was taken prisoner by Ektovians about eight years ago. They're a vile race that preys on trade routes and unarmed ships. They're despicable cowards, yet incredibly savage. We were held for almost a year. Me and my team members were subjected to…evils you don't want to imagine."

She tensed and unshed tears glistened in her eyes. "Seeing what Alonov was about to do reminded you of your captivity?" Her voice strained as compassion and dread pulsed across their link.

Unable to speak the words, he nodded.

"Were you—"

"No. We were tortured, horribly abused, but never raped."

"Then why did Alonov remind you of the past?" she asked carefully.

A lump formed in his throat, making it hard to speak. "The Ektovians had been spotted in the area, so this passenger convoy hired us to escort them. The Ektovians ambushed us, descending like locust on the unarmed ships. I'd never seen anything like it before or since."

"Did they murder all those people?" She pressed her hand to her upper chest, clearly dreading what he'd say next.

"Worse. They rounded everyone up and loaded us onto their ships."

"I'm so sorry," she whispered, encouraging him to move on.

She might not want to hear the details, but he needed to talk about it, needed to purge his mind of the festering pain. "The civilian males were sold immediately, but the Ektovians held on to us. They figured they could make more by ransoming us back to the RPDF. My team was chained right across from the cell where they kept the young females." He gritted his teeth and fought against the hate. The emotion was pointless. There was nothing he could have done then and there was nothing he could do now. "They were to be sold as breeders on planets even more barbaric than Ektovia. They were careful not to get them pregnant, but they saw no reason not to 'try them out'. I've never felt so godsdamn useless in my life."

"I'm so sorry you had to see that."

"We all went crazy the first time. Screamed and yelled, kicked and jerked on our chains until we were bloody. Jorton broke his own thumbs to get free of the chains, but it didn't help. He couldn't get past the force field in front of their cell. The angrier we got, the better those bastards liked it." He paused to lick his lips, nearly finished with the purge. "Sometimes they forced us to watch, restrained us to chairs and taped our eyes open."

"Oh my God." She wrapped her arms around him, pressing her body close.

"You'd think you'd get numb after a while, but it went on for months and I never went numb." He took a deep breath and blew it out through his mouth. There were no secrets from mates. If he hadn't told her, she might have stumbled across the images, and he refused to subject her to that.

She hasn't agreed to bond with you yet, his inner voice reminded, and his hands closed into fists.

"Why did it take so long for the RPDF to ransom you?" she whispered after a long pause.

"It's their policy never to negotiate with terrorists. There are no exceptions."

"Then how did you finally escape?"

"We didn't escape. General Paytor—this was before his promotion—defied orders and launched a rescue mission. We were under his command, and General Paytor refused to abandon us. It took him some time, but I don't think I'd be alive today if it weren't for that male."

"No wonder betraying him hurt so badly." She said nothing else for another few minutes, just stroked his chest and soothed him with her nearness. Then she stressed, "You got there in time to spare Heather. I know that's small consolation, but—"

"I'll take it." He kissed the top of her head and willed his body to relax. This was supposed to be a celebration of their success, not a morbid trip through the past. "I wanted you to know about this, so you'd understand why I found the overlord's decision to kidnap potential mates so objectionable. I don't care how he justifies it. Taking you away from your home world without permission was wrong."

She raised up again and looked into his eyes. "You never told me that before."

"I didn't want you to think I was just saying what you wanted to hear in order to endear myself to you. But I want to be perfectly clear. You have to want this as much as I do, or I won't claim you."

She smiled and kissed the tip of his nose. "That just moved you closer than you've ever been before."

He pulled her down and kissed her mouth, savoring rather than plundering. Now that his demons were exorcised he was hungry for tenderness.

After long moments of slow, deep kisses, she pushed him flat and swung one of her legs over his hips. She settled on her knees, straddling his groin, eyes gleaming with desire. "Would you like to know what I've been thinking about all evening?"

"You were with the overlord so it better not have been this." He grabbed her hips and arched, rubbing his erection against her slick folds.

She reached down and guided him to her entrance, then slowly sank onto him as she said, "I was comparing this life to the one I left behind."

"Were you now?" He rested his hands on her hips but let her move, content to watch her, fascinated by her mood.

Her breasts swayed as she rolled her hips, dragging her body up and down his shaft. "My life wasn't terrible before. I enjoyed my job and love my family. I thought that was enough for me."

"And now." Unable to remain passive, he reached up and carefully pinched her nipples.

She gasped, then shivered, moving her hips a little faster. "I didn't count on you." Her inner muscles tightened around him, caressing him with her wet heat. "You're too damn good to be true."

He sat up and wrapped her legs around his waist, then carefully rolled her beneath him. "I'm nothing special. There are thousands out there just like me." He pulled nearly out, then slowly filled her as they stared into each other's eyes. "I finally opened the message about my potential mates. You're my one and only match. You are the only female in the galaxy that can make my dreams come true." Her lips began to tremble and tears escaped the corners of her eyes. "Why are you crying?"

"That's the nicest thing anyone has ever said to me. How can I help but love you when you act like this?"

He froze, his cock deep inside her. "You...love me?"

She laughed and kicked him in the ass with both feet. "I did while you were moving. Now I'm not so sure."

He laughed, joy bubbling up within his soul. She loved him! She took one of the darkest moments of his life and eclipsed it with her light. "I love you too." He kissed her, saturating her mind with tender affection. "You have no idea how much."

She nipped his bottom lip. "Enough with the mushy talk. If you want me to believe you, show me."

He was happy to oblige.

《 》

A THUNDEROUS POUNDING on her workroom door snapped Isolaund's attention toward the portal. "Go away. I'm busy!"

"Open this door right now or I'll kick it in," Alonov's deep voice boomed through the barrier.

She wiped her hands on the towel tucked into her waistband. The formula she used to trigger the armor mutation in her karrons required meticulous attention. One drop of the wrong chemical and the formula could turn lethal. She would have to start over once she got rid of this buffoon.

Throwing open the door with an impatient sigh, she leaned her arm against the jam and muttered, "Make it quick. I have important things to do."

His huge hand grasped her throat and squeezed.

Holy fuck, had he lost his mind? She clawed at his forearm and bared her teeth as she frantically fought for breath. He always managed to confront her when Certice was not around. He just glared into her eyes. His grip was tight enough to panic her, without rendering her unconscious.

"Do I have your attention now?"

She awkwardly nodded and he slowly decreased the pressure on her throat. He didn't let go.

"Where is your handmaiden?"

"Why?" She licked her lips and blinked back the excess moisture in her eyes. She would never make the mistake of being without one of her cats again!

"When's the last time you saw her?"

"Let. Go." She shoved into his mind, triggering a sharp burst of pain.

He gasped and stumbled back, his hand finally leaving her throat. "Spare me your witchery. This is important."

"What does Arrista have to do with anything? Get to the point."

He shoved her into the workroom, then slammed the door behind them.

A shiver of fear skittered down Isolaund's back. Her mother could have incapacitated him with a thought, but Isolaund only inherited a faint echo of her mother's power. This brute could easily kill her if that was his intent.

"I found your little hostage, and was in the process of moving her somewhere safe when Arrista interfered."

He was lying. She could see it all over his face. "Heather was perfectly safe where she was. We both know what you were doing if you found her hiding place."

"Fine," he snarled. "Well, the bitch must have called for assistance because three of the Outcasts showed up and now Arrista is nowhere to be found."

Isolaund just stared at him, mouth hanging open.

"My reaction exactly. How the hells did they deactivate the cloaking shield? And how did they find the grotto so damn fast?"

She gave herself a firm metal shake and sorted through what he'd just told her. "Arrista has been taking Heather food. Are you sure she didn't just stumble upon you?"

"And the Outcasts just happened to pick that exact moment to rescue Heather? I don't believe in coincidences. Your pretty little servant is a spy."

She didn't bother to argue, but it didn't make sense. Arrista was faultlessly loyal. One of Isolaund's most powerful spells made sure of it. "Then this visit is about containment?"

He nodded. "The council can never know that those creatures breached our defenses. It would mean my position, and if I go down, so do you."

"No one will believe a traumatized human," Isolaund said dismissively, "but Arrista is a problem. If the council questions her, she'll answer honestly. That's her nature."

"Then she dies. It's as simple as that."

Isolaund glared at him. It would take years to train another handmaiden. Arrista was smarter than any other Niffal Isolaund had ever met. As well as an obedient servant, Arrista was skilled with the karrons, and had an aptitude for healing. "I'll take care of it."

"How?" he persisted. "If the Outcasts are protecting her, you won't even be able to get near her."

She hated revealing her secrets, especially to someone like Alonov. But like it or not, they were allies. At least for the time being. "I have a Shadow among the Outcasts. If all else fails, I'll activate the *lenitas* and take control."

"How in all the gods' names did you get Shadow *lenitas* into one of the Outcasts?"

She smiled, proud of her ingenuity. "Certice injected them with her bite. It was a simple procedure."

"But wouldn't the Outcast healers detect them when they treated the bite?"

"They're Shadow *lenitas*. They're undetectable to scans."

"All right." His gaze swept the length of her body. "I'm impressed."

She nodded once, acknowledging his praise.

"Take care of it quickly. I don't want this hanging over my head."

"Of course." She didn't exhale until he left, then her breath rushed out in a telling hiss. What a cluster! If the Outcasts had Arrista, she was doubtlessly another hostage. There was no way she would have left the Underground of her own free will. Mainly because she didn't have free will.

So, how could Isolaund twist this to her own advantage? Alonov was a pain in the ass. He was one of the few beings alive that she feared. He wasn't afraid of her, like everyone else. That in itself was a problem.

She paced the tiny workroom, tapping her fingernail against her lips. If she told the council Alonov was directly responsible for a breach in security, would they— No, it had to be something worse, something they couldn't tolerate. What about rape? Well, she didn't know that he'd actually raped

Heather. It sounded more like Arrista had interrupted his fun. Of course, the council didn't need to know that.

A thought occurred to her suddenly. She'd given Arrista a pendant and compelled her to wear it continually. Unbeknown to her servant, the pendant recorded whatever Arrista did and said, and everything that transpired in her presence. Isolaund only checked the feed when she had reason to be concerned, and Arrista seldom gave her reason. Had the feed caught any of Alonov's attack on Heather?

Isolaund pushed up her sleeve and triggered her subdermal control pad. She navigated through the holo-grind and activated Arrista's surveillance feed. The current image was the inside of some sort of storeroom. Had they taken away her clothes and all her possessions? Arrista wouldn't have given up the pendant without a fight. Concerned now, Isolaund rolled back the feed until two male images came into view. She continued backward until the start of their conversation. It hadn't lasted long. One was dark with sharply angled features and a cutting stare. The other was light, though he too looked stern and forbidding.

"Why'd you stop?" the light one asked. "We need to keep moving."

"Her pendant is bugged," the dark one responded. Then he lifted the chain from around her neck and slipped the decorative disk into his pocket. The image went black, and the voices grew so muffled she could no longer discern their words.

How in all the frozen hells had the Outcast known about the camera? It didn't matter. Clearly spying on the Outcasts wasn't going to happen.

She dismissed it with a shrug and regressed the feed to where Arrista entered the grotto. Alonov had Heather pinned to the ground. He held her wrists with one hand while he tried to pull down her pants with the other. Arrista dropped her tray and ran toward the struggling human. "Let her up, you beast!" She threw herself on his back, hitting at his head and clawing at his arms. Isolaund couldn't help but smile.

Alonov snarled and batted her aside as if she were no more than a nuisance. "This has nothing to do with you. Be gone!"

"You were told to leave her alone." She picked herself up and went for him again. Isolaund's smile broadened. She knew Arrista had spirt, but she'd never seen her this worked up before. Arrista kicked him in the side and slapped his face, until the general released Heather and went after her.

"You want to take her place?"

"This is wrong, and you know it."

"I know nothing of the kind. Fucking enemy females is part of war, and as long as they have my son, we are at war with the Outcasts!" He turned back toward Heather, who was now huddled against the wall.

Arrista grabbed his arm, clinging to him like a long-limbed primate. "The council forbade this!" Arrista shouted, dangling from his arm.

"Keep it up and you're next!"

Still, she didn't release her hold, so Alonov punched her in the face. Arrista collapsed and the camera pointed toward the ceiling for several seconds. The dark-haired Outcast picked her up while sounds of a fight echoed in the background. She sped up the playback, skimming through the images to make sure there wasn't anything the council couldn't see.

The attempted rape would infuriate the younger generation. And seeing him punch Arrista right in the face wouldn't hurt Isolaund's case either. But Alonov was right, however. The older set would shrug off his intolerable behavior as hazards of war. The council was split right down the middle, six young members and six old. Which meant the high councilor would decide the general's fate. Her smile was cold and calculated. And it just so happened that the current high councilor was Indrex Farr, her brother. Indrex might disagree with her on, well, practically everything, but they both agreed that abusing females for sport was inexcusable. Once the council saw the slightly edited feed, Alonov's days were numbered!

Chapter Nine

"I don't know what to do with her." Sara knelt beside the listless cub, gently stroking her dull dark brown fur. "It's been three days and she still won't eat. I can barely get her to lap water."

"She's depressed." Xorran knew he was stating the obvious, but he didn't know what else to say. Sara was tortured by the cub's decline, and he was tortured by Sara's helplessness.

"She's lonely." Arrista stood on the other side of the fence, but she'd obviously heard their exchange. "Karrons live in groups, what you call prides. The cubs are reared together. They are never alone. This is terrifying for her."

That got Sara's attention. She stood, quickly brushed off her knees as she walked over to the elf. "How do I get another cub, or two? What does Wenny need? I'll do whatever I can to provide it."

"Can't we just trap one?" Xorran asked, joining the females. "We see karrons all the time in the forest."

Arrista shook her head. "Wild karrons are very different than the ones hand raised by us. Being trained to be a 'battle cat' is a great honor." She emphasized the phrase with finger quotes, a shockingly human motion. Clearly the other females had been tutoring her. "We need one of Wenny's siblings."

"And how do we get one?" Sara asked, hope brightening her eyes.

"Let me think about it." Arrista gazed off into the distance. "It won't be easy, but let me see what I can do." She smiled and walked back toward the Wheel.

"What is she going to do, sneak back into the Underground and stick one in a bag?" Xorran shook his head, confused by Arrista's offer.

"Unfortunately, I feel the same way, but she means well."

He reached down and took her hand threading his fingers through hers. "Let's go eat while the food is still warm." He'd arrived with a tray of food, but she refused to leave the enclosure. So he spread a blanket on the other side of the fence so they could have a picnic.

With a long sigh of frustration, Sara nodded and allowed him to lead her out the gate.

They sat on the blanket and he passed her a bowl of *cyatta* stew, but she just set it down beside her and stared at the cub. "What happens to me if she dies?" she whispered. "Isolaund said she'd come get me."

"This isn't your fault, but her threats are part of the reason the overlord doesn't want you out here at night."

"You'll keep me safe." She punctuated the statement with a weak smile, but it didn't reach her eyes.

He shook his head and took several bites of stew before setting his bowl aside also. Damn it. There had to be a way to ease her fear. "She'll be fine, love. You have to believe that, if you want it to happen."

"I'm trying. Really I am." She stood and went back inside the enclosure. Wenny lifted her head long enough to identify her visitor, then went right back to...mourning. The word seemed odd, but that was what Wenny was doing. She was grieving for all the things, all the companions, that had been taken from her.

Sara lay down in the grass beside the cub. To his astonishment, Wenny crawled closer and curved her body into the warmth of Sara's. Arrista had to be right. If the cub was desperate enough to cuddle with a human, this had to be about loneliness. Sara kept using a phrase. Separation anxiety. That was what she called this, so how could they treat it. Returning her to her mother wasn't an option, but...

Good gods above, was he actually considering this? He'd have to recruit Torrin for the mission or he wouldn't even get through the door. "Sara, I'm going to run the tray back to the Wheel. Will you be okay for a few minutes?"

She didn't answer with words, just waved him on and went back to petting the cub.

He started to leave, then realized he'd about given himself away and went back and picked up the tray. She watched him closely, brows drawn together over her nose. He just smiled and hurried to the *Viper*. After depositing the tray of dirty dishes in the recycler, he went in search of Torrin.

Not surprisingly, he found the assassin working out with a spar-bot in the fitness center. Torrin paused the routine when Xorran stood beside the mat for several minutes. "Want to go a round or two?"

"No. I need to speak with you."

"Can it wait? I'm almost finished."

Xorran nodded and went to the bench lining the perimeter wall. He sat and waited while the assassin finished his workout.

The fitness center was always crowded. Xorran preferred his workouts in the privacy of his cabin, but many of the cabins weren't large enough to allow for such a preference. He had no idea where Torrin was assigned.

Finally finished, Torrin commanded the spar-bot back to its charging station and walked over to Xorran as he wiped off his face with a towel. "So what's up?"

"I need you to let me back into the Underground."

Torrin looked at him as if he'd lost his mind. "Why?"

"The karron cub needs a companion. They're not used to being alone and she refuses to eat. Needless to say, Sara is taking it badly, so I need to fix them both."

Torrin draped the towel around his neck with a laugh. "Thank the gods I'm not genetically compatible with humans."

"Will you help me?"

"Probably, but what happens after I open the door for you?"

Xorran stood up with a sigh. "I was hoping Arrista could help us with that."

An expressionless mask slammed down over Torrin's features. "Go talk to her and get back to me with a viable plan. I'm not going near that female."

What a bizarre reaction. "What did Arrista do? She's harmless."

"She's obsessed with me." He sounded horrified. "We saved her life so she feels honor bound to 'serve' one of us. Torak went back to his ship. You're taken, so I'm the lucky fool she's determined to 'serve.'"

Xorran laughed. It was obvious Torrin was anything but amused, but Xorran couldn't suppress the reaction. "So have her clean your cabin and fetch your food. How horrible could that be?"

"You have no idea. The female is...never mind. I will deal with Arrista, but in my own way and time."

Xorran held up both hands and contained his mirth to a compassionate smile. "Fine by me. I'll talk to her and get back with you."

"Check my cabin. I keep throwing her out and she keeps coming back. I've changed the security code twice. We can't figure out how she's doing it."

Okay, so maybe this was a bigger problem than he'd first thought. "Which cabin is yours?"

"Five-one-nine."

Deck five, cabin nineteen. Just down the hall from his. "Thanks."

The training center was on deck one, so Xorran took a lift to deck five. He wasn't intimidated by stairs, but he was in a hurry. Sara wasn't going to rest until this thing with Wenny was settled, and Sara had barely slept in three days. Besides, like the overlord, he didn't want her outside after dark and the sun was about to set.

He went to cabin nineteen and activated the visitor alert. Even if she was inside, would Arrista respond to the door? He had his answer few seconds later when the door slid open, revealing the elf.

"My master is training. May I take a message?"

"My master"? Holy shit, this was worse than he'd thought. "May I come in? Torrin knows I'm here."

She hesitated, but eventually stepped back and motioned him inside. Torrin's cabin was identical to his. He went to the sofa and sat. She chose the chair facing him.

He wanted to get back to Sara as soon as possible, but he couldn't help asking, "Why do you consider Torrin your master? He has made it clear it's not an honor he wants."

"We do not have a choice. He saved my life. There can be no doubt General Alonov would have killed me if Torrin had not carried me to the world above. If one saves another's life, the rescuer then owns the life he saved."

"According to whom?"

She just stared back at him blankly.

"I understand that you're grateful," Xorran tried again, "but Torrin isn't comfortable with being your master."

She lowered her gaze to her folded hands, hiding behind her pale blue hair. "Have I displeased him? I'm trying very hard to serve, but he won't tell me what pleases him."

"It would please him for you to take advantage of this opportunity and figure out what pleases *you*."

She shook her head, sounding even more miserable. "I am Niffal. We are bred to serve."

"There are no designations here, Arrista. You are free to be whatever you want to be."

Tentatively she glanced at him, but confusion still creased her brow. "But I want to be Torrin's faithful servant."

Okay, he was starting to see why Torrin was in the training center kicking the shit out of a spar-bot. Then it struck him. She literally knew nothing else. She had never longed for freedom because she had never experienced it. It was tragic. And it was far too complicated a matter to solve right now.

"Is this why you are here? Does Torrin want me to pleasure you?" Now she sounded mechanical, as if she'd shut off her personality. Her expression was equally blank. She looked like an exotic doll.

Xorran closed his eyes and clenched his fists. It didn't take a lot of imagination to figure out why she would react this way. Isolaund was such a bitch!

He cleared his throat and looked into her pastel-blue eyes. "You do not need to pleasure anyone unless you want them, Arrista. That will *never* be expected of you again."

She finally reacted. Uncertainty knitted her brow and clouded her gaze. "Then why are you here."

"I'm determined to get Wenny a companion and I need your help. Torrin has agreed to get me back into the Underground, but I'm not sure—"

"Oh sir, you cannot!" She came up out of the chair and moved toward him. "They will be ready for you now. Guards will be posted at every portal. There is no way to sneak inside."

"I have to do something." He threw up his hands, hating his helplessness. "Sara is terrified Isolaund will attack her because Wenny is so sick."

"Weniffa is not sick, she is sad, and I am working on a solution." She sounded sincere, even insistent. "You must trust this task to me."

"If we can't sneak back into the Underground, there is no way you can either. Explain your plan to me."

She looked uncomfortable, but returned to her seat and told him, "There is another cub like Wenny, one who is struggling with what is expected of battle cats. Her name is Luppa.

My sister is one of Isolaund's assistants and I can speak with her mind to mind."

"Has she agreed to help us?"

"The city is sealed," Arrista explained. "That's why your scanners did not detect us. Merella will need to venture above before we can communicate, but her work with the karrons allows her to come and go as she pleases."

"How will she know you need to talk to her?"

"Simple pulses can penetrate the shields. I have been signaling her since I left Sara. Merella knows I need her, but she must have a valid reason for going above. She will contact me as soon as she can."

"Then your sister will just bring Luppa to us? Won't Isolaund miss the cub?"

"Isolaund has been making excuses for Luppa, but she's running out of time. The Guiding Council wants to discontinue the battle cat program. They feel it's too expensive and there is no real need for battle cats anymore. They are watching every move Isolaund makes. Very soon she will have no choice but to send Luppa to the labor pool. I will tell Merella to hurry that decision along, and then she will deliver Luppa to us rather than take her to the labor pool."

He leaned back with a smile. "You win. Your plan is much better than mine."

She smiled and it transformed her features from pretty to stunning. With her iridescent skin and light blue hair she was unusually beautiful. What was Torrin's problem? Any male would love to mate with such a striking female.

If they were actually willing.

And therein lay the problem. Arrista felt honor bound to "serve" Torrin.

Xorran doubted that it would do any good, but he had to try one more time. "Heather is the only one left in Sara's cabin. Why don't you go sleep there? I'm sure Heather would appreciate the company after all she's been through."

She shook her head, looking shy again. "I must stay with my master."

Damn. Looks like Torrin had lost his cabin for a while. "Please let me know as soon as Merella responds."

"Of course."

He returned to the habitat and found Sara much as she'd been when he left her. Rather than try to get her to leave the cub, he let himself in and joined her on the grass.

"Our link is still active," she warned. "I know you're up to something."

He spread out on his back and folded his hands behind his head. The sky was so filled with stars it didn't look real. "I *was* up to something, but Arrista talked me out of it."

She laughed, sitting up so she could see his face. The cub was between them, still fast asleep. "What does that mean?"

"I was going to sneak back into the Underground and steal another cub for Wenny."

She just stared at him. "You're serious?"

"Of course. I told you I would do anything to make you happy. Didn't you believe me?"

"Yes, but...no, I guess I really didn't. I thought you meant little things like bringing me coffee in the morning. Thank God Arrista talked some sense into you. That would have been suicide!"

"If her plan doesn't work, I'm still going. I will not have you torturing yourself about this cub."

"I'm sorry. I try not to get attached, but Wenny got to me from the start. She's so sweet, so loveable. I can't imagine anyone wanting to harm her."

"I understand that, but there is only so much you can do."

She nodded, but sorrow still smoldered in her eyes. "What's Arrista's plan?"

He explained about Luppa and Merella. "Arrista seems confident that Merella can pull it off. I say we let her try."

"I agree." She paused to stroke Wenny's back, needing the contact more than the karron. "But if this fails, you must promise me you will not sneak back into the Underground. It's much too dangerous."

If he gave his vow, he would have to keep it. He considered vows sacred. "One step at a time, love. Now let's go to bed." He stood and held out his hand, but his stubborn mate lay back down.

"I'm not leaving her out here alone. She only fell asleep because I lay down with her. I'm not being stubborn. Okay, I'm not *just* being stubborn. She needs me."

He shook his head, knowing it was hopeless. "Fine. Then I stay too."

"Suit yourself."

He couldn't see her face, but he could hear the smile in her voice.

⟨ ⟩

WHEN POUNDING ON HER door awakened Isolaund she threw back the covers with a snarl. Certice leapt to the floor, echoing Isolaund's displeasure. Slipping on her robe as she ran to the door, Isolaund shouted. "Can we go one godsdamn day without you pounding on my door?"

As if to answer her question, Alonov overrode her privacy protocols and opened the door. He yanked her into her outer chamber, then kicked Certice in the face. The karron yelped and shook her head. Her momentary disorientation was long enough for Alonov to shut the door.

Then he turned on Isolaund. "You conniving bitch!"

She swallowed hard. She'd given the recording to Indrex late last night and the council hadn't met yet. How had Alonov found out?

He stomped toward her and she backed up, matching him step for angry step. "Why are you so angry?" It was a stall tactic. She had to twist this to her advantage. Maybe blame it on Indrex, claim she didn't know about the pendant and he was using it to spy on them both? Could she sell it? Alonov was no fool.

"You know damn well why I'm angry. Your sniveling brother called an emergency meeting of the Guiding Council. They're in there right now plotting my doom."

"What are you talking about?" She put on her best little-girl-lost expression, but the bastard only laughed.

"Innocence hasn't been believable on your face in years."

"Tell me what you're talking about. Why would Indrex gather the council?"

"I have people watching every access point into the central computer. One of my people detected you manipulating a surveillance feed and notified me. Before I could decide what to do with you, I hear about this meeting. Coincidence again? I don't think so!"

Damn it. She should have kept those files somewhere else. "I don't know what you're talking about. Someone must have used my access point."

He lunged for her like a raptor, fisting the back of her hair as he sneered. "Cut the shit, Isolaund. I'm not in the mood to spar with you."

She glared at him, but helplessness swelled inside her. Again, he'd caught her without the protection of her cats. And Certice had been with her this time!

She'd seen lust flash in his gaze more than once. Could she use that to shift his focus? "What are you in the mood to do?" she purred softly.

"Wring your fucking neck." He took something out of his pocket and forced it into her mouth.

The metallic taste of blood spread across her tongue and she gaged, trying to spit out the small, flat object.

Without explanation he let go of her hair and stepped back.

She spit the thing into her hand and wiped the blood from her lips. She looked at her palm and froze. Trepidation sped her pulse and knotted her stomach. "Where did you get this?"

He just leered at her.

"Where did you get this!" It was a demand this time.

"The poor creature was on its way to the labor pool. My knife was probably a mercy."

Luppa. She gagged, then ran to the sink and vomited. She had Luppa's blood in her mouth. "Why? Why would you take this out on a helpless animal?"

He laughed. "You really do love those filthy beasts more than people, don't you? And the 'why' is simple. You're going to tell your brother not to convict me. In fact you'll do whatever it takes to make sure he votes to dismiss. This was a warning, little girl. Betray me again and I'll kill them all in the most gruesome ways possible."

⟨ ⟩

WENNY JOLTED AWAKE, springing up from the ground as if it had been electrified. *Luppa. Luppa. Luppa.*

Sara blinked away sleep's haze, confused by the cub's strange actions. "Settle down, love. What's the matter?"

Go. Go now. Luppa. Luppa!

The name echoed through Sara's mind along with Wenny's fear. For half a second she thought that Arrista's plan had worked already. But Wenny wasn't excited to see her sister. She was terrified.

"Xorran. Something's really wrong."

Wenny went to the gate and butted her head against the barrier over and over.

"Luppa's in trouble. Where's Wenny's leash?"

Now! Now! Go now!

"Screw it," she muttered as she rushed over and opened the gate. "Don't run too fast or you'll lose me!"

Wenny took off like a shot, but slowed down when she heard Sara's words.

Sara ran as fast as she could, glancing back to make sure Xorran was coming. He had a pulse pistol in one hand and he looked furious. Oh well, she'd deal with his anger later.

Wenny zigzagged through the trees, leaping over any barrier small enough to clear. Sara did her best to keep up, but every time she lagged behind, Wenny paused and let her catch up. Finally Wenny veered sharply right, then stopped abruptly, calling out in a forlorn tone to make sure Sara found them. A karron cub lay in the underbrush covered in blood. Dreading what she'd find, Sara carefully felt for a pulse. When the faint beat throbbed against her fingertips, she released a grateful sigh.

"Is she alive?" Xorran asked from behind her.

"Yes, but she won't be for long unless we get some help for her." It was probably wiser not to move her, but it would take twice as long to run all the way to the Wheel, and then bring someone all the way back here.

Xorran decided for her. He reached past her and scooped up the cub in his arms. Luppa was limp, but made a soft cry. He shifted her high against his chest and Sara saw the source of all the blood.

"Dear God, someone sliced her open and just left her here to die. We need to get pressure on that wound."

He didn't react, didn't hesitate. Keeping pressure on the wound with one hand, he turned and sprinted for the Wheel. She had no hope of keeping up with him, so she didn't even try. Wenny, on the other hand, had no problem and had no intention of being separated from her sister.

By the time Sara got to the Wheel, Xorran was nowhere in sight and guards surrounded Wenny, who was snarling and snapping at anyone who came close to her. She'd made it within feet of the ramp. *Go, Wenny.*

Sucking in a much needed breath, Sara commanded, "*Dez-tee!*" Wenny looked at her and Sara raised her right hand, palm out.

Wenny whined but sat down and stopped growling. Her mental barrage, however, grew louder. *Luppa. Luppa. Luppa.*

Sara knelt in front of Wenny and took her face between her hands. She looked deep into her blue eyes, determined to make her understand. "You can't go in there, baby. My mate is taking care of Luppa. They will do everything they can to make her better."

Wenny hung her head and whined, the plaintive sound breaking Sara's heart.

"Can you control her if I let you onboard?"

She looked up and found Kage standing a few feet away, his expression intensely concerned.

"Yes, sir." She struggled back to her feet, still slightly out of breath. "I'm not sure I can get her back into the enclosure and even if I do, I'm not sure she'll stay."

"Then come on."

Seriously? He was going to let her walk through the Wheel with Wenny?

"Tell her to stay by your side. If she moves away from you, I'll stun her."

She noticed the pulse pistol in his hand for the first time. She switched back to Sarronti and said, "They're going to let us go to Luppa, but you have to stay right by me. Do you understand?"

Wenny be good. Go. Go now.

Sara took three slow steps to see if Wenny understood. The cub advanced as fast as Sara, but not a step farther. "Good girl."

Wenny turned her head and licked Sara's hand.

Gasps and shocked expressions followed them all the way to main medical. Kage took them to the small waiting room just outside the clinic, then said, "Let me find out what's going on before we waltz in there with a battle cat."

"Of course, sir."

He frowned. "You were calling me Kage the other night."

"It made Xorran mad," she admitted.

He chuckled as he scanned open the door. "All the more reason to do it."

She sat on the chair closest to the door and Wenny sat on the floor at her feet.

Luppa soon?

"Yes, baby. You'll see Luppa soon." *Please, God, let her still be alive,* she finished silently, then looked at Wenny, afraid the cub heard her thought. Wenny didn't react, so Sara tried to relax.

There was no way she was going back to Earth, and the thought didn't even scare her anymore. She was already more invested in this world than she'd ever thought possible. She'd managed to meet the most amazing male in any star system, and hopefully she'd have two karrons to care for now instead of one.

Odd that it took this sort of crisis to make her secure in her feelings for her mate. As with everything they'd faced so far, Xorran dealt with this calmly and authoritatively. She wasn't sure what she'd done to deserve him, but she would be eternally grateful.

Wenny was starting to get restless, when Xorran came out of the clinic. He sat down next to Sara and gave her a hug, then reached down and stroked Wenny's head. "Dr. Foran has her stabilized, but she lost a lot of blood."

"Can't they just put her in one of these regeneration tubes?"

"They need to scan a healthy karron before the regen unit can work. Luppa's too damaged right now to—"

"Hello." She motioned toward Wenny. "Healthy karron at your service."

"Why didn't I think of that?" Without another word he stood and went back inside the clinic.

When he returned a few minutes later, he had Dr. Foran with him. Foran had an injector in his hand.

"Wait. Let Wenny see Luppa and you won't need to sedate her. I'll just explain what you need her to do."

The doctor looked at Xorran, clearly thinking Sara was hysterical.

"My mate can talk to animals, what else do you need to know?"

"I'd feel much better if it was on a leash." He eyed the cub distrustfully. "Do you realize how many karron bites I've had to repair?"

"She won't leave my side," Sara assured him.

With obvious reluctance Dr. Foran led them through the door. A stunned hush fell over the clinic as they crossed the room. "She's back in isolation," Foran directed.

Wenny started to lunge ahead, but Sara said, "Wenny," in a warning tone and the cub immediately repositioned at Sara's side. "Good girl."

Luppa lay on a treatment table, an IV catheter in her neck. Her laceration had been sutured and her breathing appeared less labored. Wenny went up to the table, but the surface was too high for the cub, even when she went up on her hind legs. Seeing the dilemma, Dr. Foran lowered the table to Wenny's eye level. Wenny lay her head next to her sister's and made a sound Sara had never heard before. Luppa stirred for a second, then went limp again.

"Wenny, come here." With some reluctance, the cub returned to Sara's side. "Luppa is still very sick. Do you want to help her?"

Yes. Do anything.

She looked at the doctor. "How does this work. Does she need to lie in the regen unit?" That might be really frightening. Maybe she should let him sedate Wenny.

"If she holds sill enough, I can scan her right here. But she cannot even blink or the scan will fail."

She knelt and explained this to Wenny. She wasn't sure the cub understood until her eyes widened and stopped blinking. "She's ready." Sara crawled backward, out of the way.

"Most people can't pull this off, but..." He activated the scanner and red bars of light crisscrossed and scrolled the entire length of Wenny's body. Sara thought it was over and started to tell Wenny she could move, when the glowing bars reversed direction and repeated the sweep. She held her breath, praying for a miracle. "Unbelievable." Dr. Foran breathed a sigh of relief. "It worked."

Wenny did good?

Happy tears blurred Sara's eyes. "Oh, baby, Wenny did very good!" Still on her knees, she crawled over and gave the cub a hug.

Luppa heal?

She didn't want to make false promises, so she looked at Dr. Foran. "Will you be able to regenerate her now?"

"I don't see why not. The unit works flawlessly with anything for which it has an accurate pattern. Thanks to your extraordinary pet, I now have an accurate pattern."

"Wenny's not my pet," she objected. "She's my friend."

The doctor just smiled, then went to go load the pattern into the regen unit. A few minutes later they moved Luppa into the unit and started the regeneration cycle.

"How long will this take?" Sara asked no one in particular. Xorran stood next to her and Kage was lounging against the wall near the door.

"Several hours, at least," Kage told her. "You should go get some sleep."

"I can't leave Wenny. She's still too upset."

He just chuckled and looked at the cub, then Sara heard his voice inside her mind. *Wenny, your mistress needs to get some sleep. Why don't you stay with me so her mate can put her to bed?*

Wenny got up and moved over to him, then sat and looked at Sara expectantly.

"That's cheating," she complained. He was clearly a skilled telepath. What else could their mysterious leader do?

"Take your mate to bed," Kage ordered.

Xorran scooped her up in his arms and headed for the door, "With pleasure," he said as he passed the overlord.

"You can put me down now," she said once they'd reached the main corridor.

"And have you run back in there? Not a chance."

She smiled and looped her arms around his neck. "Have it your way."

"Oh, I intend to." He grinned, making sure she knew exactly what he meant.

"I'm supposed to sleep, not share pleasure with you," she pointed out, but already her body was warming, preparing for their joining.

"You sleep better after we've shared pleasure. Can you deny that it's a fact?"

"I could, but why would I want to? After a day like this I need a release, or two," she said with a mischievous smile.

"Happy to oblige," he promise, and lengthened his strides.

Chapter Ten

Refusing to be rushed, Xorran ignored Sara's urging to hurry and undressed her slowly. "Wenny has monopolized your attention for the past three days. Right now you're mine, and I will not share you with anyone. Even your 'baby.'"

She stilled, her expressive gaze searching his. "Have I been that bad?"

He framed her face with his hands and kissed the tip of her nose. "Your tender heart is one of the reasons I love you so much. But I've earned a little selfishness."

"I agree. You've been faultlessly supportive through all of it."

So she slowed down, undressing him with the same caressing care that he used to rid her of her clothing. When they were both naked, she turned and prepared to crawl into bed. He encircled her waist with one arm and drew her back against his front.

"I want to touch you first," he whispered into her hair.

"You can't touch me in bed?" But she didn't pull away. Instead, she wiggled her bottom against his thighs and pressed more firmly against his aching cock.

She was so tiny he could tuck her head under his chin. It made kissing challenging, but she didn't seem to mind. He ran his free hand over her breasts, loving the weighty feel of her soft flesh. Her nipples pebbled beneath his lightest touch and she was always wet when he eased his hand between her thighs. The pull was heightening their attraction, he knew. Still, he suspected she would always be a highly responsive mate.

He lingered over her nipples, rolling them between his fingers and thumbs and gently pulling on the sensitive peaks.

"I like it better when you use your mouth." She arched her back, pushing against his fingers

"I know, but you're going to stand there and let me touch you."

She chuckled. It was a familiar game. "Why would I do that when what I really want is your hard cock deep inside me?"

"Because you're not getting my cock until you come for my fingers."

She shivered, then moaned. "How do you do that?" she whispered. "I don't even like dirty talk and yet with you I can almost come just talking about coming."

He laughed. "We'll have to put that to the test some time."

"But not tonight?" she asked hopefully.

"Definitely not tonight." He kicked her feet apart, making more room for his hand between her silky thighs. Thrilled by the wetness already gathered on her folds, he pushed two fingers up inside her.

She sagged against him with a moan. "That feels so good."

"Glad to hear it." He moved his fingers in and out, savoring her heat and the slick slide of her obvious arousal. "Now come for me." He found her clit with his thumb and ensured that she obeyed. It took about two seconds and her inner walls were rippling around his fingers. "Good girl."

She laughed and caught his wrist. "I say that to Wenny when she obeys me. You need to find another phrase."

He picked her up and placed her on the bed, not bothering to pull down the covers. He crawled onto the bed and stretched out on his side facing her. "Now you're going to do it all over again because I want to watch your face when you come."

"Oh you're in one of *those* moods." She even managed to sound annoyed, but mischief and anticipation lit her gaze. "Go on," she teased, "Get it over with. Give me orgasm after orgasm until I pass out from the pleasure."

He laughed. "Such a sacrifice."

He slipped one arm under her neck and cupped her breast as his mouth covered hers. Her taste was addictive and he intended to fully indulge his habit tonight. He explored her soft lips and the velvety interior of her mouth before curving his tongue around hers. As always, she returned the kiss with equal fervor, one of her hands combing through his hair.

I love you, Xorran. Never doubt it. She emphasized the thought with tingling affection.

And I love you. He pushed his devotion into her mind.

Once they were bonded the exchange would be effortless. Sharing thoughts and feelings would be as natural as breathing. Once they were bonded. The phrase echoed in his mind and a pang of frustration disturbed his arousal. He hadn't asked her about accepting his claim in over a week. There had been too much conflict in their lives, and he'd been content to support and comfort her. She was his only match, but she had many more matches to choose from. Was she considering anyone else?

"Where'd you go?" she asked when he pulled away. "Suddenly I couldn't sense you anymore."

"The transfer link is starting to deteriorate." It was, but he'd also withdrawn from the link, not wanting her to sense his frustration. "It will need to be reestablished if we want to continue sharing emotions."

"Ooor," she drew out the word, then smiled. "You could just create the real link. I know I'm ready. Aren't you?"

He tensed. Had she heard his mental grumbling? He did not want to pressure her in any way. This had to be something she wanted desperately. "There's no rush, Sara. I know you're still—"

She pressed her fingers over his lips, stemming his words. "As long as I can still interact with my family, there is nothing more to decide. I know exactly what I want, and I'm looking at him."

This was what he'd wanted, what he'd literally ached for ever since he met her. So why the hell wasn't he claiming her? "The past few days have been extremely stressful. Are you sure you're not just..."

"Just what?" She sat up and crossed her arms over her breasts. "Are *you* having second thoughts?"

"Gods no! I just want this to be perfect. I don't want you to feel pressured or rushed."

She smiled and pressed her hand against the side of his face. "Sweetheart, you won my heart when you took off your shirt and used it like a blanket on Wenny, but you earned my loyalty and unconditional trust when you promised to sneak back into the Underground to steal another cub. You are the most selfless person I've ever met and I'd be a fool not to hold on to you with both arms." She bent down and kissed him before adding, "I want to bond with you, Xorran Entor, and someday—in the not too distant future—I want to have a bunch of babies that look just like you."

His heart was beating so fast it stole his breath. He sat up and wrapped both arms around her. Their mouths found each other and fused while their tongues sensually danced from mouth to mouth.

I will spend the rest of my life making you happy, he vowed. *I will protect you with my life and love you in this life and the next.*

Without separating their mouths, she crawled onto his lap and wrapped her legs around his waist. *I accept your claim, my love. Form the soul bond. I am and will always be your mate.*

Say please, he ordered playfully and her joyful laughter sounded in his mind.

He lifted her slightly and found her wet core with the tip of his cock. She quickly folded her legs beneath her and brought her body into better alignment with his. Slowly, oh so slowly, her snug heat enveloped his rock-hard shaft. It felt so good, so right, as if a missing piece of his soul had been finally snapped into place. She paused with his entire length inside her, savoring the fullness, the completeness. Her pleasure heightened his, but the link was definitely fading.

Ride me, love. I need to concentrate.

My pleasure, she assured and began to move, rolling her hips while flexing her knees.

He focused on her mind, on what was left of the transfer link. He needed to dissolve it completely before he formed the soul bond. One cleansing pulse was all it took to eradicate the connection, and suddenly he was alone.

She tore her mouth away with a gasp. "I didn't realize how isolated I was without you in my mind. I don't ever want to feel like this again."

"My thoughts exactly," he whispered and began to form the much more complex link.

Apparently sensing his distraction, she braced her hands on his shoulders and went back to pleasuring him with her amazing body. Her breasts rubbed against his chest and her inner muscles hugged him firmly with each slow stroke. His arousal generated the extra energy he needed to form the bond, but it was damn distracting. He wanted to lay her back across the bed and regain control of their joining. He wanted to take her fast and hard, proving once and for all that she was his.

But first he had to finish the link. He sucked in a breath and closed his eyes. Weaving the strands of energy into an intricate pattern that would help them locate each other at even great distances, he gradually linked his soul with hers.

So much better, she whispered as their emotions began to flow again. She was curious about how much different this would feel from the transfer link, and more than a little frustrated by his distraction.

Almost done, he assured her as he secured the final few strands. Now all he had to do was anchor each side. Should he warn her or just do it?

Just do it.

He chuckled. Apparently, the link was fully functional. She'd heard his thought without his assistance.

Here we go. Without pause, he blasted the connection with a massive pulse of energy.

She cried out and shuddered, clutching his back as her body shook. "You could have mentioned that it would hurt like hell."

Rather than point out that she'd asked for it, he grabbed her hips and flipped her onto her back. "So much better," he echoed her words as he started to move in earnest.

She raised her legs high against his sides and arched into each of his downward thrusts. Their joining grew almost frantic after that. He filled her completely with each demanding stroke and she clawed at his back. His gaze bore into hers as emotions flowed freely across their soul bond.

Not only could he feel her emotions now, he could feel her physical sensations. He was filling and being filled. And pleasure passed between them in a continuous loop. Her sensations heightened his as his strengthened hers. Faster and faster he pumped, desperate for completion, yet never wanting it to end.

She suddenly arched and cried out sharply, her strong inner muscles massaging him as distinctly as any hand. Lost to everything but the pleasure, he threw back his head and closed his eyes. He drove into her one final time and released his seed in pulsing spurts.

Aftershocks caused her to shudder and moan, or maybe she came again. He couldn't tell which and didn't really care, as long as she was satisfied.

Carefully rolling them to their sides, he gave in to the creeping lethargy.

"And I have to put up with *this* for the rest of my life?"

His eyes flew open and she laughed.

"Your sense of humor can be exhausting," he grumbled.

"Sorry, love. It's a package deal."

"We all have our burdens to bear." Despite his desire to savor the moment, his eyelids drooped.

"Hey. I'm the one who's supposed to be sleepy, and I'm ready to go again."

"Catnap," he promised, and she gradually relaxed in his arms. Soon they were both sound asleep.

⟨ ⟩

SARA STOOD JUST OUTSIDE Wenny's habitat three days later watching the cubs frolic through the grass. They ran and wrestled, growling playfully. Luppa was fully recovered from the brutality of General Alonov, and Wenny was thrilled with the company.

While Sara and Xorran had been out in the forest searching for Luppa, Merella contacted Arrista. Only the news wasn't good. Merella explained that Isolaund finally buckled to the Guiding Council's pressure and sent Luppa to the labor pool. Merella had been tasked with delivering the cub, but she never made it to her destination. Alonov ambushed her in the corridor and snatched Luppa right out of her arms. Then he knocked Merella unconscious. The bastard was good at beating up females. When Merella woke up someone had carried her to her room and it was too late to inform Isolaund of Alonov's bizarre behavior. Arrista told her sister what had happened on their end, and Merella agreed to allow Isolaund to believe the cub was dead. The bitch deserved that much at least for her callous behavior.

"They both look wonderful," Xorran said as he walked up beside her. "Why are you scowling?"

"I was just thinking about Isolaund and all the other cubs she's tossed away like garbage because they weren't vicious enough to be useful."

He placed his hand on the small of her back, a gentle reminder that she wasn't alone anymore. "Arrista insists that she had no choice, but I'm with you. Isolaund only cares about Isolaund."

Truer words were never spoken. "She might have saved Wenny, but Luppa is proof of her ruthlessness." That bitch needed to die. Sara sighed at the blood-thirsty thought. Dwelling on the elf was a waste of energy. Sara had too much to be grateful for to let Isolaund taint her happiness.

Xorran slipped his arm around her waist and pulled her to his side. "This was supposed to help with your preoccupation, not give you someone else to worry about. You're turning into a helicopter parent."

She laughed at the human phrase. "Where did you learn about helicopter parents?"

"We uploaded Earth's entire internet to our database."

She'd known they had a lot of information on humans, but that was surprising. "You guys are thorough, aren't you?"

"Among other things." He smoothly guided her away from the fence and deeper into the surrounding forest. "Did you enjoy talking with your brother?"

"*Brothers,*" she corrected. "Jose was with Tim when Kage arranged the call. And yes, it was wonderful to talk to them."

"Are they horribly upset that you're on another planet, in another star system?"

She shrugged. "It's a longer commute than Lunar Nine, but going off-world was unavoidable as soon as I volunteered for the battle born program." They strolled through the trees for a moment in silence, content to be together. "Where are we going?"

"Nowhere in particular. I just wanted to change your view."

She deserved that. She had been a little obsessed about the cubs.

"Have you seen Arrista at all in the last few days?" His tone was casual, but an odd combination of emotions surged into her mind as he asked the question.

"Once or twice in passing. Is there a problem?"

"She's latched onto Torrin, insists on 'serving' him."

She stopped walking and faced him. "That's not good. Is Torrin taking advantage of her?"

"Just the opposite," he assured her. "Torrin has been avoiding her, but she's persistent. It's almost as if she's...compelled to serve someone and Torrin just happens to be there."

"The Sarronti use a strict caste system, and Arrista is on the bottom rung. This is likely just culture shock."

He nodded, but still looked concerned about their new friend. "Can you spend time with her? See if you can help her accept her new reality."

Sara smiled. "Of course. I've had some experience with that sort of transition. I'll do whatever I can."

"Good." He took her hand and started walking again.

Soon they came to a bend in the river. The clear green water flowed swiftly here, the rushing sound soothing. Turquoise grass lined both banks and tall, leafy trees created a tranquil, secluded feeling for the small clearing. Sara drew him over to a waist-high rock formation.

If her mate was feeling neglected, she needed to give him some attention. "Give me your shirt." His gaze narrowed, so she added, "Please."

Watching her closely, he removed his uniform top and handed it to her. "Now, do I get yours?"

"Nope." Instead she pulled off her shoes, and took off her pants. He followed every move she made, but said nothing else. She spread his shirt across the relatively flat bolder, then hopped up onto the rock. "Come here." She crooked her finger and he quickly stepped between her thighs.

"I like where this is going." He caught her hips and slid her forward, but waited for her next directive.

"I'm here for you, love, now and forever." She accented the promise with a tingling wave of affection. "Do anything you want. I'm yours and yours alone."

The End – For Now…

Next Up

Outcasts Book Four

Featuring Torrin and Arrista

Did you love *Tracker*? Then you should read *Heretic* by Cyndi Friberg!

Restless and embittered by an abusive past, Arton the Heretic finds himself in a battle of wills with Lily, a gorgeous geneticist. She holds the key to the future of his people, but she was brought to this savage world against her will and that's an insult she'll not soon forget. Their attraction is instantaneous and intense, yet each has valid reasons for mistrusting the other. He wants her, is consumed with the need to claim her, but he can't focus on the future until he deals with the past.

Read more at www.cyndifriberg.com.

Also by Cyndi Friberg

Alpha Colony
Untamed Hunger
United Passion
Unwanted Desire
Uninhibited Fire

Battle Born
Enforcer
Fearless
Defiant
Triumphant

Beyond Ontariese
Taken by Storm
Operation Hydra
City of Tears
Mystic Flame
Fire Pearl

Consort

Dream Warriors
Dream Warriors Gareth
Dream Warriors Ryder
Dream Warriors Kane
Dream Warriors Chaos
Dream Warriors Collection

Outcasts
Heretic
Tracker

Therian Heat
Therian Priestess
Therian Prey
Therian Promise
Therian Prisoner
Therian Prize

Watch for more at www.cyndifriberg.com.

About the Author

Passionate Sci-Fi with a touch of danger and a whole lot of sass.

USA Today Bestselling Author: When my parents realized I had an aptitude for storytelling—okay, even at an early age I was a consummate liar—they encouraged me to find constructive ways to put all that "creativity" to use. I wrote my first novel when I was in junior high school. It was a typical teenage girl's fantasy about being kidnapped by a sexy rock star, finding out he was really a misunderstood millionaire's son, and living happily ever after with the reformed rebel. Rock stars led to vampires and vampires to outer space. Not sure how that happened, but I sure love it there.

Now I spend my days, and many of my nights, trying to keep up with the characters springing to life within my mind. I find creative ways of avoiding errands and housework because

I can't drag myself away from the drama unfolding in my latest story. And every day I thank God I was able to quit my day job and actively pursue my dream!

I love to hear from readers and do my best to respond as quickly as possible.

Email me at: author@cyndifriberg.com

Facebook Page: https://www.facebook.com/fribergc/

Twitter: https://twitter.com/Cyndi_Friberg

Read more at www.cyndifriberg.com.

Printed in Great Britain
by Amazon